Please return on or before the latest date above.
You can renew online at *www.kent.gov.uk/libs*
or by telephone 08458 247 200

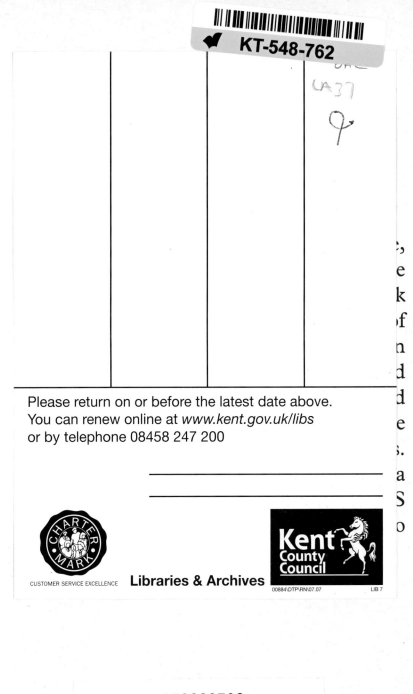

OPERATION IL DUCK

OPERATION IL DUCE

OPERATION IL DUCE

by

Charles Whiting

Dales Large Print Books
Long Preston, North Yorkshire,
BD23 4ND, England.

British Library Cataloguing in Publication Data.

Whiting, Charles
    Operation Il Duce.

A catalogue record of this book is
available from the British Library

ISBN   1-84262-245-5 pbk

First published in Great Britain 1975 by Seeley Service and Co.

Published in Large Print 2003 by arrangement with
Eskdale Publishing

Dales Large Print is an imprint of Library Magna Books Ltd.

Printed and bound in Great Britain by
T.J. (International) Ltd., Cornwall, PL28 8RW

THE DESTROYERS: OPERATION IL DUCE

'There isn't much to be frightened of. We've come to the epilogue – the biggest turning point in history. The star is dark.' *The Italian Duce, Benito Mussolini to his mistress Claretta on the night of 24/25 July, 1943.*

Operation Mincemeat~
Phase Two (July 1943)

The Rescue (12th Sept. 1943)

ITALY

YUGOSLAVIA

Pescara

CORSICA

Gran Sasso

Rome

Pratica di Mare

La Maddalena

SARDINIA

SICILY

••)••)• The destroyers' route
→ — Skorzeny's route

SECTION ONE:
OPERATION MINCEMEAT

'For my money, Ike, if anyone can pull it off, it'll be the Destroyers. I say – let 'em get on with it!' *General Patton to General Eisenhower, July, 1943*

CHAPTER ONE

Somewhere a church clock struck twelve. The muffled sound of a shunting engine at St Pancras station was the only other noise to disturb the night. In the big camouflaged staff car, the Destroyers slumped in silence, waiting for the man they had been called back from leave to meet. An elderly war-reserve policeman moved up the street with officious deliberation. In the rear-view mirror they caught brief glimpses of his black-out torch as he flashed it in the shop doorways.

Commander Mallory, dressed in civilian clothes, whispered to the Destroyers, 'Don't say anything if he stops.'

When the policeman came level with the big Humber parked under the unlit gas lamp he flicked on his torch. 'Good evening,' he said warily. 'Everything all right?'

For a moment no one spoke. Then Mallory pulled out his special pass, gave the policeman a brief glance at it and then indicated with a jerk of his head that he should move on.

The policeman straightened up and saluted. 'Sorry to have bothered you, sir. Didn't know who you was.' He touched his helmet. 'Well, good night, gentlemen. Looks as if it's gonna get worse before it gets better.'

'You can say that again, mate,' Stevens commented sourly as he plodded on.

Ten minutes later Commander Mallory broke the silence. 'There he is,' he said. 'All out.'

The Destroyers needed no urging. They jumped out behind their leader, the one-eyed Lieutenant Crooke, as the ancient Rolls came to a stop on the other side of the road. Commander Mallory bent down and whispered something to the driver of the Rolls. Two men got out of the back and the car moved off.

As the car drew away, Stevens said to Gippo, 'You know who that is, you ignorant nig-nog?'

Gippo shook his head.

'You wogs don't know nothing. That's Spilsbury – Bernard Spilsbury, the feller that used to do the murderers before the war!'

'And the other bloke?' Peters, standing behind Stevens, asked. 'Who's he?'

Stevens looked at the middle-aged man standing beside the white-haired pathologist, who was perhaps the world's leading specialist in his field. 'Search me.'

The other man looked up and down the street and then took a large old-fashioned key out of the pocket of his trousers and fitted it into the door of the house in front of which they had alighted.

It opened with a rusty squeak and the Destroyers followed the two men inside. An odour of formaldehyde and ether met them. When they were all inside he locked the door again.

Sir Bernard Spilsbury tugged at his high wing collar. 'Shall we go down now?' he asked. 'It's very late.' Without waiting for an answer, he turned and started to walk down a long dark corridor.

'Who's the other jerk – the guy in the fancy pants?' Yank asked.

'That's Mr Purchase,' Crooke whispered to Jones, the American member of the Destroyers, known without much originality as 'Yank', 'the coroner for this district.'

'But what the heck have we got to do with the sawbones?' the American asked. 'Jesus Christ, can't Naval Intelligence find any other way of wasting time?'

Sir Bernard Spilsbury stopped. The coroner hurried forward and opened the glazed door which barred their way. A wave of cold air came out. *'Scheisse!'* Thaelmann, the communist member of the Destroyers, cursed in German. 'It's cold.'

'Here we are, gentlemen,' Sir Bernard said, 'the borough mortuary.'

Crooke looked round the high room, filled with strange-looking drawers which reached right up to the roof. Mallory caught his look and smiled understandingly. 'Perhaps, Sir Bernard,' he said to the pathologist, 'you might explain to my men why we are here?'

Spilsbury turned to the Destroyers. 'Gentlemen, I'm getting too old to be spending more time than is necessary in mortuaries, so I'll make it short. Last winter the Commander here and a colleague of his in Naval Intelligence asked me to find a body which looked as if it might have suffered death by drowning. With the aid of Mr Purchase I achieved that end and the body was duly used for a rather dubious intelligence mission which the Commander had code-named – somewhat drastically – Operation Mincemeat.'

Mallory interrupted. 'I must remind you that what you're hearing now is absolutely top secret. The body kindly supplied by these two gentlemen was used to create an imaginary major in the Royal Marines named Martin. Well, our fake Major Martin was fitted out with false papers which indicated that when our forces in the Med invade Europe it will be in Sardinia. Thereafter one of our subs dumped the body off Spain so that the Germans or their Spanish stooges would be able to pick it up. That was in April this year.'

'But it's July now, sir. How do we know that Jerry found the body?'

'I was present at the burial of the body in Huelva a few days later.'

'Pretty neat. But how do you know that they've swallowed the bait?'

'We don't, of course,' Mallory said. 'Not for certain, anyway. But our latest information is that Admiral Canaris and Field Marshal Rommel have already visited Sardinia and that the 1st Panzer Division, one of the Boche's crack units, is on its way to Greece. Obviously to stand by for an invasion of Sardinia. We're keeping our fingers crossed, and Admiral Godfrey has empowered me to take the op a stage further.' He turned to the pathologist. 'Now, Sir Bernard, what are your conclusions?'

Sir Bernard gripped the lapels of his black jacket and cleared his throat, as if he were about to address a jury. 'I have examined the bodies as instructed. All three of them have injuries which are consistent with their having fallen from aircraft – and ones which will be easily recognisable – ruptured spleen, broken ankle bones, a burst lung.' He turned to Purchase. 'William, I wonder if we could see the bodies now?'

Purchase walked over to the nearest drawer and pulled it open. A long shape covered by a sheet came into view accompanied by a little cloud of icy air. He tugged at a second drawer. Another body covered by a sheet appeared. And another. Purchase pulled back the sheet on the first body. A pale face above a camouflaged paratrooper's smock appeared. 'Trainee from the 6th Airborne Division. Killed at Ringway Jump School last week.' He cleared his throat and smiled thinly. 'Roman-candled, they call it.'

Mallory pulled back the sheet on the second body. A brutish face was revealed, on which thick, bushy eyebrows grew almost together. Resting across the breast was a big hand on which was tattooed a regimental badge and the legend 'Death or Honour'.

'Well, he got the death but without very much honour,' Sir Bernard commented. 'He was killed in a tavern brawl two weeks ago. With one of our American cousins.' He sniffed. 'Struck over the head with a blunt object – a beer bottle to be exact.'

'Thank you, sir,' Mallory said.

Purchase pulled back the third sheet. *'Oberleutnant* Schmitz,' he explained, 'late of the German *Luftwaffe*. Bailed out on a tip-and-run raid over Folkestone last month. Unfortunately his parachute did not function.'

The Destroyers stared at the young face of the dead German. Like the other two bodies he was clad in a camouflaged British paratrooper's smock.

Mallory turned to them. 'Take a long and careful look at their faces,' he ordered. 'Take your time and fix them in your minds.'

While the Destroyers stared at the three dead men, Mallory took out a small can from the pocket of his suit. 'We've had an afterthought, gentlemen,' he said to the two doctors. 'We came to the conclusion that they could have walked around in their socks at their base in North Africa. Soldiers do, you know.'

Sir Bernard and Mr Purchase nodded, but

said nothing.

'So we assumed that they would have collected the local dust on their clothing – and in particular in their socks.'

Sir Bernard pursed his lips. 'Very likely, Commander Mallory. Very likely.'

'Thank you, Sir Bernard. At all events I have had this little can of dust sent from Eisenhower's HQ at Algiers. The experts tell me that it is easily recognisable as the local stuff. So if we could get the boots off, gentlemen?'

'I wish you could have thought of this before,' Purchase said irritably. 'It took us quite some time to dress them in their present clothing.'

He left the room and returned in a few moments with an electric fire which he plugged in and positioned near the young paratrooper's feet.

Gippo licked his lips and swallowed thickly as the seconds ticked by. Then something began to drip. Gippo turned green. He thrust a fist into his mouth. 'I'm coming sick, sir,' he said, 'very sick in the stomach.'

CHAPTER TWO

'Char?' Gippo asked, his face still pale green, as he came through the glass door of Room 39, bearing his tray.

'Yer, real sergeant-major's tea,' Stevens added, following him into the centre of Naval Intelligence operations. 'The duty bloke gave me a couple of tins of milk – none of yer condensed stuff.'

'Thank you, Stevens,' Mallory declined the proffered cup. 'I think I'll stick to my scotch.' He refilled his tumbler from a silver hip flask.

'What about a wad, sir?' Stevens persisted. 'Spam and bully. Don't worry, sir,' he added, 'the nig-nog hasn't had his paws on them.' Gippo was in no way offended; he and the cockney were the closest among the Destroyers.

'I'm sorry you had to go through all that,' Mallory said, 'and even more sorry that I had to call you all back from your well-earned leaves so suddenly.'

'Not more sorry than me, sir,' Stevens said

21

pausing in the middle of a huge corned beef sandwich. 'I'd just got me pants off and was telling her she'd better have a good look at the floor because she'd only be seeing the ceiling for the next seventy-two hours when those sodding redcaps of yours started hammering at her door.'

Mallory smiled. 'Stevens, we have no desire to hear about your dirty doings,' he said patiently.

Crooke flashed a warning look at Stevens and tugged at his black eye-patch. 'Commander Mallory, can't we get on with it?'

Mallory gazed at the little team, which had been carrying out the DNI's most secret and dangerous missions since Crooke had brought them out of the Cairo Military Prison the year before. Stevens, the smart little cockney, who had been sentenced as a deserter after a year of masquerading as Colonel Stevens, running a large scale black market operation in the desert. Gippo, the black-eyed, half-breed who claimed to be an illegitimate descendant of Lord Kitchener and whose long fingers had landed him in jail after being wounded three times with the Eighth Army. Lone Star Alamo Jones, the Texan mercenary, a ruthless yellow-faced killer, who had been sentenced to death for shooting German POWs after being ordered to escort them to the rear. Peters, the former regular Coldstream Guards sergeant-major, erect and hard, who had been stripped of his rank and imprisoned because he refused to go into action with inexperienced officers. Thaelmann, the German communist, silent and bitter, who had fled Dachau Concentration Camp to continue the fight against fascism until he had been put into Cairo Military Prison on a charge of treason. And Crooke, the one-eyed CO of the Destroyers, who had lost his eye and won the Victoria Cross during the commando attempt to kill Rommel in 1942. After he had recovered from a serious wound, he had refused to remain in a desk job in London; he wanted action again. But he had gone about it the wrong way. He had struck the Deputy Commander Home Forces on the nose. In the ensuing court-martial he was reduced in rank from colonel to second-lieutenant and posted to Naval Intelligence.

'Of course,' Mallory broke his own reverie. 'Well, you heard my little account of Operation Mincemeat in the morgue. Now Admiral Godfrey has decided to take the op a little further. As soon as our chaps and the Yanks land in Sicily, Admiral Canaris will know that the late Major Martin was used to fool him about Allied intentions. But we think we can hoodwink him a little more.'

He walked to the curtains which covered the top secret intelligence map on the wall and drew them. 'Ignore the measles,' he said, indicating the rash of blue and red marks on it. 'They show the Boche secret weapon sites we're interested in.' He tapped Sicily. 'In exactly seven days the British 8th Army under General Montgomery and the US 7th Army under General Patton will invade Sicily. As soon as the island is taken, we'll invade Italy proper.'

'So we're going to invade Europe this year after all?' Peters exclaimed. 'The Reds forced our hand in spite of the Caucasian Fox business?'

'Not really. The Italian invasion will be a limited operation.' He nodded towards Yank. 'Your compatriots don't want to make Italy the major effort. They're still for France. Now the most likely spots for our invasion of southern Italy are Salerno near Naples, Reggio just across the straits from Sicily and Taranto on the east coast. All of them are obvious places where the Boche would expect us to land. They are all ports which we'll need for our build up. So the plan is this. Husky – the code name for the plan of the Sicily invasion – envisages a drop by the First Airborne Division, presently in North Africa. It's our intention to let one of the pilots involved miscalculate and drop a stick of paras just over Reggio, where the Italians or the Boche can't help but find them.'

'The men we saw in the mortuary?' Crooke asked.

'Yes. As Sir Bernard Spilsbury said, all of them have injuries which will fool the enemy into believing that they met their death due to a failed para-drop.'

'And?' Crooke prompted.

'We're going to supply them with fake material, indicating that the same 1st Airborne will be used for another drop once Sicily is taken. Indeed we will supply the dead chaps with the watered-down details of the Baytown plan, the 8th Army's cover name for the capture of Taranto. The result – we hope – will be that the Boche will think the First's target will be Taranto.'

'But say Jerry has tumbled to the fast one you pulled on him with your Major Martin?' Stevens objected. 'Won't he give this plant the thumbs down?'

'Right,' Mallory said and lit another

cigarette. 'Sometimes, Stevens, you're too damned smart for your boots.'

'We could always swap jobs, old chap,' Stevens answered airily, assuming that fruity upper-class voice which he had used so successfully in his long-time impersonation of Colonel Stevens, his 'pound-notish' voice as he called it.

'That's just how we're expecting them to react,' Mallory said, ignoring the last remark. 'But this time we're going to ring the changes a little. This time the plants will carry the real site of the 1st Airborne's landing, which will be Taranto. We are hoping the German will buy the whole bag of tricks and that Taranto won't be defended when the First Airborne Division sails into the port.'

'*Sails!*' Stevens echoed the word.

'Yes, sails. That's the final touch. Just in case the Germans don't get the word and decide to defend the likely para-drop sites on the heights outside the port.' Mallory yawned and looked at his watch. It was nearly three. 'Gentlemen,' he said, 'I think that's about all for tonight – or should I say this morning. You had all better get off and try to get a few hours' sleep because we'll be flying from Croydon at ten hundred hours.'

'Where to, sir?' Peters asked.

'To Algiers. We're going to put Operation Mincemeat, phase two, to the big brass – to General Eisenhower himself.'

CHAPTER THREE

But Mallory was mistaken. They did not take off at ten hundred hours next morning. The RAF Anson which was to fly them to North Africa developed an engine defect and it took some strong words from Admiral Godfrey and considerable wire-pulling before they were finally fixed up with a Sunderland flying boat which was flying to Gibraltar to pick up some Polish VIPs. At dusk the four-engined seaplane took off from Plymouth and made a long flight into the Atlantic to avoid the German Focke-Wulfs stationed on the French coast before the Canadian pilot finally set course due south-east. As dawn started to break, they crossed the coast of Portugal. A little later as Gippo and Stevens were helping to prepare breakfast in the little blacked-out galley, the Rock itself finally hove into sight. The young

Canadian pilot brought the plane down through the fog and made a neat touchdown just off the entrance to the harbour. Slowly he followed the radio beam through the gate into the harbour, filled with shipping intended for the great invasion, until they came to a stop at a bollard close to the harbour wall.

The Destroyers stared through the portholes at the gleaming white houses and the busy life of the port, while Mallory and the crew prepared to go ashore in the launch which was now chugging out to meet them.

'I'm going to do the rounds and see if I can bum a lift for us to Algiers,' Mallory said to Crooke.

'Who are you going to try?' Crooke asked.

'For a start Simpson, the AOC. I know him vaguely. And if he won't play ball, I'll try the bar of the Rock Hotel. That's where all the big shots hang out. I might be able to thumb a ride there.'

Suddenly Crooke decided that this was as good a moment as any to ask the question which had been plaguing him ever since they had first been introduced to Sir Bernard Spilsbury and had learned about Operation Mincemeat. 'Mallory,' he said softly, 'what is our part in this op?'

'Not very much,' the Commander answered. 'You're going to be nursemaids to those bodies – the special equipment cases we loaded at Plymouth – once they've been dropped to ensure that they get to the right destination.'

'And that is?'

'Oh, nobody important,' Mallory said airily.

'Who?' Crooke persisted.

'Canaris – Admiral Canaris, the head of the *Abwehr.*'

Two hours later the fog began to thicken again. One by one the great World War One warships and the tankers and the troop transports disappeared into the swirling fog. In a matter of minutes what looked like an impenetrable white wall faced them through the ports. They were alone on the gently swaying water, cut off from the world. All was silence save for the mournful call of a ship's foghorn somewhere outside of the harbour.

Time passed slowly. The Yank found some cards and started to try to teach the others how to play poker. Gippo and Stevens got bored and as was their habit started to wander about the Sunderland in search of what they could find. 'Finding it before it's lost,' as the Yank commented sourly. 'Thieving bastards!'

Crooke walked aft and stared thoughtfully at the three zinc chests, containing the bodies of the dead men. What had Mallory meant by 'nursemaids'? If they were to be dropped by plane, how could they 'nursemaid' them to Canaris? And where was the white-haired spymaster himself? At his headquarters in the Tirpitzstrasse in Berlin? Or on one of his constant journeys? A lot of questions, and no answers!

Suddenly through the porthole he caught sight of a strange black shining object, outlined against the white wall of fog. The thing looked like a great fish, but the white blur which gazed at him from behind the big goggle was a human face! Then it vanished.

Crooke ran back to the cabin. 'Stand to,' he shouted. 'There's something out there in the water!'

The Destroyers' reaction was instantaneous. A big .45 appeared in Yank's hand, Thaelmann and Peters grabbed their stens. But nothing happened. The seconds passed in silence and slowly the tension slackened. 'I don't know, sir,' Peters said, blinking a little with the effort of staring so hard at the white wall of fog outside, 'I can't see anything.'

Crooke bit his lip. Slowly he lowered his .38. 'Perhaps you're right,' he began. 'I thought…'

Suddenly there was a dull boom, muffled by the fog. A second later a vivid red flame split the white clouds swirling all around them. The flying boat rocked violently. From the galley there came the sound of pots clattering to the floor. 'What the hell's going on?' Stevens cried, coming out from behind the curtain, wiping his hands on a towel.

'You, Yank, Peters and Thaelmann, out on the wings,' Crooke yelled. 'Stevens, Gippo get that porthole open. Whatever the hell's out there, it's not on our side.'

Everything was controlled, yet frantic activity as the Destroyers took up their battle stations. Crooke swung the door of the Sunderland open. Thrusting his revolver in his pocket, he reached up and grabbed the ladder which led to the wing as another explosion rocked the flying boat violently. He threw himself flat on the wing and peered down at the water some nine feet below. Moments later he was joined by

Thaelmann. 'The Yank's taken the other end,' he whispered and levelled his sten. 'What's going on, sir?'

He didn't have to wait long to find out.

'Look,' Crooke grabbed his arm in warning. A dark shape appeared directly below them, raised a hand out of the water and tried to fix something to the flying boat's hull. It was a limpet mine! Crooke raised his revolver. But Thaelmann was quicker. A salvo of 9mm slugs ripped into the man below. The glass goggle shattered and the white blur of a face disappeared in a spiderweb of broken glass. The man threw up his hands in mortal agony. Blood stained the surface of the water a bright red for a brief instant. Then he was gone. Behind them the two men could hear the rattle of the Yank's sten.

'Look out there!' It was the Yank.

They swung round to see a rubber-clad monster flopping along the wings, a pistol in its hand. Crooke fired and missed. Thaelmann pressed the trigger of his sten and their attacker was blasted over the side, as if punched off the wing by some gigantic invisible fist. And in that same instant another explosion rocked the Sunderland. Before Crooke could catch himself, he had slithered over the edge of the wing and was in the water. 'Are you all right, sir?' Thaelmann shouted, peering down at him from over the wing.

But Crooke's attention was wholly devoted to the dark shape flashing towards him through the water. He caught a glimpse of a face behind a mask, and the silver sheen of a knife. He rolled to one side as the knife threshed the water inches away and the impetus carried his attacker under. Crooke struck out at the disappearing rubber-helmeted head and missed. The attacker did a lightning somersault in the water, came up behind Crooke and grabbed his foot. Struggling frantically Crooke went under. Down and down he was dragged and felt his head begin to spin and his lungs threaten to burst. Desperately he kicked out with his other foot and felt his boot hit something hard. The grip was released and he shot to the surface, gasping for air. But his assailant was at him again in an instant, although now he was minus his knife. Crooke caught a quick glimpse of the thick rubber tube thrust in the man's mouth and smashed his elbow into the masked face. Its impact was deadened by the glass goggle, but it achieved its aim. He grabbed quickly at the man's airline which came out with a plop. The face behind the goggle was suddenly contorted, but he recovered quickly and brought up his knee which caught Crooke behind the legs. A sickening pain shot through his body. Desperately he thrust out his hands and clawed at the man's mask. At the same moment he felt his back hit something. It was the bollard to which the Sunderland was tied up. His fingers found the edge of his attacker's mask and in an instant he had ripped it off his face. Using the last of his strength, Crooke swung his assailant round and smashed his head against the rusty bollard. A stream of blood shot out of his nostrils and he opened his mouth to scream. But Crooke did not give him a chance. Exerting all his strength, he grabbed the man's head and thrust him under water. Frantically the man struggled to escape. Grimly Crooke held him down. Slowly the struggles began to weaken. Then they stopped altogether. Crooke waited anxiously a moment. Then with a soft plop the corpse appeared on the surface and lay there spreadeagled on its face in the dirty water of the harbour, which was now calm once more.

CHAPTER FOUR

The Sunderland's cabin was crowded with harbour officials, armed redcaps and anxious naval officers, all staring down at the dead rubber-clad figure sprawled out on the floor.

Biggs, who Mallory had introduced to the Destroyers as 'head of naval security', nodded and said grimly, 'That's another of the bastards, an Eyetie.'

'A wop?' Yank said in surprise.

'They're not all ice cream merchants, you know,' Biggs said. 'Like all you chaps in the desert think they are. There are some brave bastards among them.'

Crooke sat slumped in a canvas chair watching the scene apathetically, not yet recovered from his ordeal.

'The Jerries call them "wave riders",' Biggs went on. 'We call them – for the want of a better word – "torpedo-men". They hit us first last December and we killed a couple of them with depth charges. We go over the inner harbour with depth charges regularly at night,' he added by way of explanation. 'Back in May they had another go. Without success. But today they really put one over on us. This bloody fog helped of course. Three tankers and a Navy oiler down the drain.'

'Do you know where they come from?' Mallory asked.

'Yes, from so-called neutral Spain. The Eyeties have got the tanker *Olterra* in the Algeciras harbour over the straits on the Spanish side. Their merchant marine scuttled it in 1940. Last year the ship was put under what the dagoes call "neutrality guard". A lot of drunken Spanish recruits, easy to bribe and even easier to fool. Under the leadership of a chap called Licio Visintini they bribed the dagoes to let them build a secret base into the *Olterra*.'

'What do you mean a secret base?' Mallory asked.

'Well, they cut a twenty-five-foot long section in the steel bulkhead, separating the bow compartment from a small cargo hold. This they hinged. That done they bribed the dagoes to let them clean the trimming tanks – or at least that was the excuse they gave. The Spanish agreed. So the Eyeties pumped out the forward tanks till the bow rose high

36

out of the water. A couple of days later – when the guards were kipping – they cut a door into the side of the ship, opening into the bow compartment below the normal waterline. This they hinged to open inward in a way that only a diver could find it. The trimming tanks "cleaned", they flooded the bow compartment again. But now the hold was dry and filled with human torpedoes – twenty-two-foot torpedoes with detachable warheads. They're steered by a couple of men, who sit astride of the things. The Eyeties call them *Maiale* which means pig in their lingo – and they are really pigs to catch. Wearing rubber suits and a kind of mobile breathing apparatus so that they can come in under the surface, they launch their torpedoes and then set off on a nice little orgy of destruction with limpet mines, like the one you have just witnessed.'

'But how do they get back to their base?' Mallory asked.

'In theory they're supposed to swim back. It's not far, but I think myself the buggers don't expect to get back. It's a one way journey. At least for that poor sod it was.'

Mallory nodded and then turned to the rest of the onlookers. 'Gentlemen, I'm sorry but I'm afraid I'm going to have to chase you out. I have some confidential business to discuss with Commander Biggs here.'

Slowly the others filed out to the waiting launch.

Mallory turned to Thaelmann. 'Check if they're gone,' he ordered.

Thaelmann followed the visitors. A couple of moments later he came back and held up his thumb. 'All clear, sir.'

Mallory turned to the security man. 'All right, Biggs, I'm not telling you much – save this. We're here on a special operation, which is of vital importance to the war effort. I'm anxious to know whether our mission has been compromised in any way by this attack.'

Biggs pulled the end of his nose thoughtfully. 'As I've already said, we've had these attacks before. And their target was pretty obviously the ships in the harbour. As far as I read it, they just happened to chance on your flying boat because of the fog. But we'll soon see.'

He stuck the tip of his shoe under the dead Italian and turned him over with a grunt. The Italian fell with a wet sound on to his back, his dark eyes wide open and staring into nothing.

He bent down and unzipped the rubber suit.

'Italian ID card,' he said, drawing out the dead man's identity document. He glanced at it and passed it on to Mallory, who in turn handed it on to the Destroyers.

'One photo. Probably Mama and the bambini,' Biggs said. 'Real big lungs those Italian women have,' he added with a leer. 'It's all that pasta they eat.'

Mallory glanced at the poor photo of a young woman holding two neat black-suited boys by the hands. He passed it on to the others without comment.

Biggs dug deeper. 'Ship identification chart. Probably had to learn the silhouettes of the ships of our Mediterranean Fleet.' He glanced down the black outlines of the British ships quickly and whistled softly. 'Look at this,' he said, handing the chart to Mallory. 'The *Ark Royal*. The Eyeties had big ideas if they thought they were going to sink her.' He fumbled in the dead man's pocket once again and dug up a couple of small keys, a few crushed scraps of paper and a thin tube of brown tablets. 'Dope,' he explained. 'Supposed to pep the bastards up before they go into action.' He straightened up again and said to Mallory. 'Nothing there that I could see which might compromise your mission, whatever that may be, Commander.' He slapped his hands together as if by this gesture he could wipe away the dead man and all the trouble he had caused for the port's security force. 'Well, I think I'd better be off. I'll send a boat out for the stiff.'

'Thank you, Biggs,' Mallory said, 'I'll walk you to the exit.' He had already seen the look in Thaelmann's eyes.

Biggs gone, he walked hurriedly back to where the Destroyers were standing.

'What is it?'

'This.' Thaelmann handed the identification chart to him. The dead man – presumably – had drawn a rough pencil sketch of a skull-and-crossbones on the back of the chart, and on the skull-and-crossbones were two letters 'MD' – the initials and insignia of the unit patch he had designed himself for his little force, 'Mallory's Destroyers'.

'Balls,' he said, forgetting his Etonian reserve.

CHAPTER FIVE

'Hi,' General Eisenhower, the Allied Supreme Commander in North Africa, greeted them in his big office in the Hotel King George halfway up the cliff overlooking Algiers, as if they were old friends. 'Nice to see you fellers. I've heard a lot about you.'

To the Destroyers' surprise, as they stood stiffly to attention, he got up from his desk and insisted on shaking each one by the hand. The man who was one day to be the President of the United States was working hard at being a true democrat – a 'GI general', as some of the troops called him.

'Georgie,' he said to the tall three-star general, who sat looking moodily out of the french window, 'these are the guys from the special outfit I was telling you about.'

George S Patton, commander of the US 7th Army, swung round in his chair and stared at the Destroyers. Finally he said in a strangely high-pitched, almost feminine voice, 'I don't goddam know why we've got to have the sonuvabitch navy in on this! And goddamnit, if we have, why the goddamn Limey navy!'

With that he swung his chair round to face the window again and took out a big cigar which he lit with an aggressive flourish, his West Point class ring sparkling in the rays of the sun as he did so.

'Now, don't be like that,' Eisenhower said with a shake of his head. 'All right,' he turned to the Destroyers again, 'tell me what happened at Gibraltar, Commander Mallory.' The grin that was known to millions of cinema-goers throughout the Western hemisphere was absent from his face.

Swiftly Mallory briefed him, while he listened in silence. When Mallory was finished, Eisenhower said quietly, 'I originally sent a signal to London to ask you fellers to come and see me because of this cover operation you were doing for *Husky*. What do you call it – Operation...?'

'Mincemeat,' said Mallory.

'That's it. Well I kinda buy the first part – Major Martin and all that. But I'm worried about this second deal with the dead paratroopers. What say the Krauts buy it at its face value and are waiting for the 1st Airborne in Taranto? And now this business at Gibraltar on top of it! I don't know. Firstly your mission is dubious and now we could assume that it has been compromised to boot.'

'I don't think so,' Mallory said. 'The way I read it, the Italian Secret Service has been warned by the *Abwehr* to expect activity by my Destroyers now that it's obvious we are going to attack somewhere in the Med. Perhaps as a routine thing, all Italians and Germans involved in clandestine operations have been warned to keep a lookout for us? Perhaps the dead chap had attended a briefing on my men and had sketched the insignia to while away the time.'

Eisenhower turned to the commander of the 7th Army. 'What do you think, Georgie?'

General Patton chomped at his big cigar. 'I don't know,' he said. 'The Krauts are not dumb. They've proved that often enough to our cost. But you Destroyers look a pretty tough bunch of boys. For my money, if anyone can pull it off, it'll be this crew. I say – let 'em get on with it!'

'Okay,' Eisenhower made up his mind. 'You win, Commander Mallory. You can go ahead with your mission. But I wouldn't like to be in your shoes if you screw it up.' He pressed a button on his desk and an attractive red-haired girl appeared from an adjoining office.

'Kay, would you take these fellows over to the OSS section. They've not got a vehicle. And the best of luck, gentlemen.'

As they followed the girl out, Stevens nudged Gippo and whispered, 'Did you get that, Gippo – gentlemen! You know what that means when the brass hats call us gentlemen – us, the scum of the British Army?'

'Yes, when they are doing that, we are falling out for trouble.'

'Who was that?' Crooke asked after the girl had dropped them at the American OSS section HQ outside the town.

Mallory dabbed his brow with an elegant silk handkerchief. 'Kay Summersby. British citizen – or was. Joined Eisenhower as his civvie driver in forty-two. Now she knows more about his plans than any half-dozen generals you can think of. A lot here don't like her. They say she's an SIS plant on Eisenhower to keep tags on him for the British.'

'And is she?'

'Well, I don't...' Mallory didn't finish.

A big crew-cut American in tan uniform

with the gold leaf of a major at his collar came out of the inner office, hand extended, teeth flashing in a smile of welcome.

'Welcome aboard, Commander Mallory,' he said in a pleasant New England accent. 'Sorry to keep you waiting.'

They were ushered into a small office, which was probably no different from any other in the HQ, save that the blinds were drawn and there was a brownish lump of what looked like toffee on the major's desk.

'Yeah,' the American said, following the direction of the Destroyers' gaze. 'PE – plastic explosive.' He picked up the lump of toffee, which gave off an evil smell. 'We have to keep the stuff on General Donovan's* orders, although it gives me a helluva headache. In case we're hit by the Krauts, the office – and presumably me too – is supposed to go skywards. But please sit down.'

Mallory took out a cigarette and fitted it into his holder. 'I presume you're au fait with the background of this operation, Major?'

'Operation Mincemeat? Sure. The only

*General 'Wild Bill' Donovan was the commander of the OSS.

45

problem is how my organization can help you.'

A tough-looking, master-sergeant, with a .45 strapped to his belt, poked his head through the door. 'Yeah?' he asked.

'Bring him in,' the Major said.

A moment later the master-sergeant reappeared, pushing a short, skinny, dark-skinned man with a great hook of a nose in front of him. The man's head was completely bald and although he wore GI uniform, his olive-drab fatigues bore no badges of rank. The little man's eyes were dark and furtive, a mixture of menace and peasant cunning. 'Okay, buddy,' the master-sergeant said, 'stand to attention when you address the Major. Get it?' He emphasised his words by poking a thick forefinger into the little man's ribs.

The man said nothing.

'Let me introduce you to the latest recruit to the OSS,' the Major said, waving a hand at him. 'Gi-Gi Cicconi, commonly known as Giggles.'

The little man pulled a sour face but still did not speak.

'A month ago Giggles felt he owed something to Uncle Sam and realised it was his patriotic duty to do something for the

46

cause of democracy. He volunteered for duty with the US Army – from Sing-Sing! Now on parole, courtesy of the OSS, Giggles is a member of the United States Army.'

Giggles, who looked as if he had never smiled in his whole life, made an obscene gesture with his thumb. 'In a pig's eye,' he snarled.

The sergeant dug him in the ribs. 'Watch the lip, buddy! Or you can get in a load of trouble in this man's army!'

Mallory broke the Destroyers' slightly bewildered silence. 'Fine, Major. But what has this – er – chap got to do with us and our op, if I may ask?'

'Quite a lot. Our little friend is going to help you on your mission. He's going to be your conducting officer in Italy.'

'Stone the sodding crows!' Stevens gasped.

'You see,' the Major added, 'Giggles Cicconi is a former soldier in the Mafia!'

CHAPTER SIX

'All right, Major, let's have the story,' Crooke said after the Destroyers had filed out together with the master-sergeant and the latest addition to their team.

The Major smiled. The Major seemed always to be smiling. 'It's simple,' he said. 'You guys don't speak Italian – and you don't know the country. You don't have any contacts there either. So it seemed to me, when General Eisenhower gave me the order to help you in your mission that I had to find someone who could fill those gaps. Result – Giggles, a guy who's only happy when he's killing someone.'

'I hope you fully appreciate the situation, Major,' Mallory interrupted him. 'Crooke here and his men are going on a very dangerous mission – risking their lives. They've got to be able to rely one hundred per cent on the people they work with. They've got to know everything about them. You understand that, I'm sure.'

'Of course, Commander. And as far as

Giggles goes, it's a long story. But I'll make it as short as I can, though I can't promise to make it sweet.' He settled back in his chair. 'In the thirties the two big wheels in the Mafia underworld were Lucky Luciano and Meyer Lansky, the only non-Italian in the Brotherhood.'

'I've heard of Luciano,' Mallory said. 'He's in jail for drug-peddling, isn't he?'

'He was, but that's classified. At all events he's out because his buddy Lansky volunteered to help us if the Federal Government would spring Luciano.'

'How could a thug like Lansky help the US Government?'

'Operation Underworld, Commander,' the American said. 'I know it sounds crazy but the two of them are presently organizing their contacts in Sicily and Italy to help us on the invasion.' He held up a big hand to stop Crooke's protest. 'I can guess what you're gonna say, but those two mobsters have a helluva lot of contacts all over the south, right down to the smallest one-horse wop village. Let me give you an example of the way the Mafia can work. Vito Genovese – who was the hood who ran the Mafia in New York state before the war – lammed out of the country because he was a murder

49

suspect and ended up in Italy. In Rome, to get in well with the fascists, he bought the local party a new headquarters to the tune of a quarter of a million bucks. Okay, the deal paid dividends and he got to know the Duce himself. Early this year Mussolini complained to Vito that a New York Italian publisher, a guy named Carlo Tresca, was putting out a newspaper which was really slanging the Duce. Ten days later Tresca was gunned down by unknown assailants at the corner of 5th Avenue and 15th Street. I think you'll agree that the killing is a pretty impressive testimony to the way that the Mafia operates on *both* sides of the Atlantic.'

'All right,' Mallory said, 'but where does Giggles fit into this?'

'Small time operator. Born in the Bronx. Reformatory as a kid for petty theft. The usual career of a small-time hood after that until the Mafia took him up as a torpedo in New York, but he never got beyond the rank of soldier.'

'Soldier?'

'Yeah – a sort of enlisted man in the Brotherhood. The Mafia's as rank conscious as the regular army. Well, in 1940 Giggles got caught running teenage girls across the Texan border for the Mexican cat houses.

Apparently the greasers like blonde Americans. The FBI caught up with him and he got fifteen to twenty years in Sing-Sing. That's where Lansky found him. Now he's on parole to us with a chance of having his sentence reduced if he produces on this mission.'

Mallory lit another cigarette. 'Nice sort of a chap to have around, eh? Reformatory, extortion, white-slave trade.'

'Yeah, the kind of guy we could do without under normal circumstances,' the Major agreed. 'But you couldn't exactly call Operation Mincemeat normal, could you?'

'But how do we know that we can trust your Giggles?'

Before the Major could answer Mallory's question, Crooke cut in. 'The only safeguard we've got is this.' He slapped the .38 at his hip.

Mallory nodded. 'You're right, of course, Crooke. Better put one of your chaps to watch him all the time.' He turned to the Major. 'Have him billeted with the Destroyers and as an extra precaution, what about having that bruiser of a first sergeant keep his eye on him too.'

'You mean Bull? Sure, he's the best top kick I've ever worked with – and he hates

Giggles' guts.'

'Good,' Mallory said. 'Now what's the situation?'

The Major rose and pointed to the big map of the Mediterranean on the wall behind him. 'You're to go in with the first wave of the British First Airborne on the night of 9–10 July. The Division will drop in the hills beyond Avola – here. Your plane will continue to fly on over Sicily, providing the flak doesn't get you.' He smiled again. 'And drop here.' He touched the map again with his forefinger. 'Just beyond Reggio di Calabria.'

'What are weather conditions going to be like?' Crooke asked. 'The Destroyers have made para-drops before, but I don't suppose that little crook has.'

'No, he hasn't – and the weather isn't going to be too hot. The met boys forecast heavy seas and a thirty-five-mile-an-hour wind. Not too good eh?'

The two British officers nodded their agreement.

'I'm afraid we've just got to take that chance,' Mallory said. 'One final question, what do you hear from Rome?'

The Major's face brightened again. 'Our man in the Vatican radioed last night that

52

Canaris is in the capital. He's conferring with General Amé, the head of the Eyetie Secret Service.'

'Good, so we know that the man to whom the – er – goods are going to be delivered will be on the spot.'

'Yeah and we know from another source – Fairy Queen – that he's staying in Rome till at least July.' The American grinned mischievously.

'What's the joke?' Crooke asked.

'Excuse me. I was just thinking of Fairy Queen. That's the code name for our agent who works as a chauffeur for the German Military Attaché's assistant. As well as being an agent for Amé, reporting on the Germans, he also reports on both sides for us.'

'So what,' Crooke said.

'Nothing really, except he's a queer – hence his cover name Fairy Queen.'

Crooke snorted and Mallory grinned at his impatience. 'Don't take on so. Pansies have a place in this world too, especially if they spy for us.' His face grew serious again. 'S-o, our man's in Rome. All we've got to do is get the goods to him on time so that he can make his evaluation for the Führer.' He rose to his feet. 'Well, Major, I suppose that's it, isn't it?'

'There's only one catch, Commander,' the American said as they moved towards the door.

'And that is?'

'It's the 21st Transportation Wing – the guys who are going to fly your group of the 1st Airborne to Sicily. They're green – awfully green. Their pilots have never flown a combat mission before.'

CHAPTER SEVEN

In a gigantic V that stretched for ten miles the Dakotas carrying the 1st Airborne flew over the Mediterranean. Behind them in another V came further C-47s towing the gliders. All in all some ten thousand men of the veteran Airborne Division were now safely in the air, flying towards Sicily. At first the Destroyers, the pockets of their jump smocks bulging with maps and money and escaping gadgets, had joked a little, bursting now and again into ribald laughter at Stevens' accounts of his experience in Algiers' red-light district. But now, an hour later, they sat quietly in their bucket seats, each man sunk deep in his own thoughts, their eyes continually flicking over to where the three dead men sat wedged in their seats.

'They give yer the sodding creeps,' Stevens drew his gaze away from the eerie sight and shuddered. 'Bloody wrong it is. It ain't right, Yank.'

The Yank, who had been ordered to keep an eye on Giggles during their stay in North Africa, said, 'Yeah, it is kinda weird, sitting here with them stiffs. What do you say, wop?'

Giggles did not answer. His face was impassive. The only sign of his nervousness was the way he kept tumbling two silver half dollar coins back and forth through his skinny fingers.

Crooke yawned and stared out of the open door. He could just make out the dark silhouette of another Dakota, but the trails of fiery red sparks on all sides indicated that they were in the midst of a great armada of planes.

Time passed slowly. Midnight came and went. An hour went by. Crooke noticed that the chill in the base of his back which indicated that they were flying high was beginning to vanish. They were coming down. The atmosphere within the plane began to get close and stuffy as it had been on take-off in North Africa.

Crooke craned his neck to look out of the doorless exit. He could see the dark outlines of the other Dakotas as they snuggled together into a tight combat formation. They were perhaps some fifteen hundred feet above the sea and he could tell it was rough. Down below the light displayed by one of the Royal Navy patrol craft, which he knew acted as a check point for the Transportation Wing's inexperienced navigators, was bobbing up and down like a cork in a mill race.

The crew chief worked his way down the green-lit interior of the plane, a canvas bucket in his hand. His face was unnaturally pale in the eerie light. Carefully avoiding looking at the three dead men swaying woodenly in their seats now with the increased air turbulence, he said thickly, 'If any of you men want to puke, here it is.' He held up the bucket. 'We'll be crossing the coast of Sicily in about two minutes. The pilot reckons there'll be no flak. Down there our people are in position, ready to give your guys and the leading seaborne troops covering fire…' The words died on his lips as the Dakota shuddered violently. Swiftly he grabbed at a seat as the plane dropped a hundred feet. 'Jesus,' he cried, 'what the hell was that?'

The answer to his question was not long in coming. Flak rapped at their egg shell of metal and perspex. The plane shuddered again. A blinding red light momentarily filled the open exit. The blast of the exploding shell struck them in the face and knocked the breath out of their lungs.

His eyes wide with horror, the crew chief screamed. 'It's our own ships!… *Our own ships are firing on us!'*

Crooke sprang to his feet. Holding on as best he could in the violently jolting plane, he peered out. Below him the invasion fleet had been galvanised into frantic activity. Searchlights flicked on and swayed back and forth, lighting up the tight transport formation in their beams. Multiple machine guns started to chatter and white tracer stitched through the night air. Throughout the fleet the heavy ack-ack opened up. Crooke looked no longer. 'Get down on the deck,' he shouted. 'And hold on tight!'

The Destroyers needed no urging.

As Crooke pushed aside the frightened

young crew chief, he caught a glimpse of the first Dakota going down in a fiery trail. A moment later another disappeared in a burst of red and yellow flame. He worked his way up the fuselage, thrust aside the curtain to where two young pilots were crouched over the controls. 'Give an identification signal!' he yelled above the roar.

The senior pilot did not seem to hear. His whole attention was concentrated on the flak streaming up towards them from all sides. Suddenly he became aware of Crooke's presence and swung round, his eyes wide with terror. 'They're slaughtering our guys out there!' he screamed. 'Slaughtering them!'

'Give the recognition signal,' Crooke yelled. 'The signal, damn you!'

As the Dakota lurched violently once more, the pilot pointed to his ears.

Crooke understood. He grabbed the spare flying helmet hanging over the back of the bucket seat and plugged the R/T in. 'The signal,' he explained once more. 'Give the recognition!'

'Too late,' the skipper's voice crackled through the earphones. 'We ain't got a chance in hell now! I'm turning back!' Even the distortion of the R/T set could not hide the panic in his voice.

'You stupid bastard!' Crooke yelled at the top of his voice. 'It'll be just the same whether you go on or go back! You'll have to run the gauntlet of this stuff!'

But the skipper was not listening. His eyes were fixed with horrified fascination on the plane in front of him. Flak had sliced it neatly in half. Now the two halves were swirling down to the shore like grotesque metal leaves. Crooke craned over the pilot's shoulder and waited for the white flowering of the crew's parachutes. None came. Moments later the first half hit the ground in a burst of bright red flame. The pilot's face puckered up, as if he were about to cry. 'That was Joe Yagga – my buddy,' he whispered hoarsely over the throat mike. 'Joe dead – on his first mission!' As he spoke he jerked at the plane's controls. Crooke braced himself as the transport started to swing round. 'But you can't go back,' he yelled. 'You can't!'

But the pilot was not even listening. His eyes were fixed hypnotically on the instruments; his sole concern was to get out of the range of the deadly barrage which filled the sky all around them. In front of

59

them another Dakota took a direct hit. Its two wings folded up immediately and tore off the tailplane on their way. Great chunks of metal debris came flying towards them. As the pilot took violent evasive action, para after para tumbled from the stricken plane, kicking and twisting wildly as they fell to their deaths, their chutes burning on their backs.

Holding on grimly with one hand, Crooke pulled out his pistol and thrust it against the pilot's temple. 'You're going on,' Crooke yelled. 'I'm going to count to three and then I'll fire. One – two–'

'Ben, get the bastard!' the pilot cried to his companion.

Without looking round, Crooke rammed his elbow into the other man's face – hard. The co-pilot screamed as his nose broke.

'All right,' the skipper yelled, his voice hysterical, 'you limey bastard! But if I ever get out of this mess alive, don't let me ever find you alone without that goddamn revolver!'

Thirty minutes later they were crossing the straits which divide Sicily from the mainland. They had left behind the survivors of the 21st Transportation Wing. The red light next to the door began to glow. 'Four minutes to go,' the crew chief said, rising to his feet and peering out of the exit. Crooke nodded to his men. The Destroyers rose. But Giggles remained seated, flicking the two half dollars through his fingers in monotonous silence.

Stevens nudged the Yank. 'Okay, you spika da lingo. Tell George bloody Raft there that we're off.'

The little man glared at him.

'All right,' Stevens said easily. 'I know yer love me, now on yer feet!'

'Yeah, haul ass!' The Yank leant power to his command by thudding his booted foot into the other man's leg. He got up quickly.

Crooke, crouched by the door, looked out. By the light of the moon he could see the farms and fields below, shrouded in the blackout. Nothing moved. But on the horizon behind them he could still make out the faint pink glow of the assault barrage on the Sicilian beaches.

The alarm bell rang and the little light changed to green. Time to go. One by one the Destroyers started to hook up their static lines, which would jerk the canopies out of their parachute packs as they dived clear of the plane.

61

'Stand by to go,' the crew chief yelled above the howl of the wind.

'Okay, the stiffs first,' Crooke said. 'Yank, you and your friend give me a hand before you hook up.'

'Hell, no, I'm not gonna touch a stiff,' Giggles said, speaking for the first time.

'Knock it off,' the Yank growled, picking up the first body and manhandling it to the exit. 'If the CO says you pick up a stiff, you pick it up. And fast!' His voice dropped menacingly. 'You read me, buddy?'

'Yeah, I read you, *buddy*,' he hissed. 'But I won't forget.' Without another word, Giggles bent down and lifted up the next dead man.

Yank heaved and the young parachute trainee who had been killed at Ringway disappeared into the darkness. The *Oberleutnant* followed, then the old soldier killed in the brawl.

Crooke clipped on his static line. The young crew chief raised his thumb. He cupped his hands over his mouth. 'Okay, let's go!' he yelled.

Crooke jumped. The wind struck him in the face almost physically. He was thrown round and his head struck the tail wheel of the Dakota. Stars exploded before him and he yelped with pain. For a moment he blacked out completely. When he came round, he was swinging gently from side to side, above him the parachute shrouds a tangled mess and beyond that the black silhouette of the plane. It was blowing hard. Just as the Major had predicted it would do. Hastily Crooke began to pull at the shroud-lines. A small tumbledown farm loomed up to the left. Crooke fumbled with the lines again. He didn't want to land there. If the place had dogs, they'd have half of Southern Italy awake in no time. A violent gust of wind caught hold of him and he felt himself being driven down the valley at full speed. Instinctively he caught his breath as the ground loomed up ever nearer. A large wood of mixed firs and pines came rushing at him. He pulled up his knees to protect his belly, but before he could cover his face with his arms, he had crashed through the top branches. There was the sound of heavy twigs breaking. A branch snapped back and hit him in the face. His nose was filled with the smell of resin. Then he fainted again. How long he was unconscious he did not know. When he came to all was silence save the sound of the wind in the trees. He might well have been alone in the world.

Slowly he began to assess his position. He had landed on top of a tree and was hanging with his back against the trunk, his weight supported by his entangled parachute. He reached carefully for his commando knife, and twisting round so that he faced the trunk and could use his knees and feet to gain support, he began sawing through the entangled mess of shroudlines. One by one they snapped until finally he was free. A few moments later he was on the ground. He pulled out his pistol and took off his parachute gear to reveal the civilian clothes below.

Still there was no sound to indicate the presence of either friend or foe. Crooke hesitated. He pulled out the little clacking device – a spring-loaded metallic gadget which gave off a hoarse sound somewhat similar to the croak of the bullfrog. He pressed it gently. The resultant noise seemed like that of the grandfather of all frogs. For a moment he stood there, listening to its sound die away. Then it was answered to his left – perhaps a hundred yards away. He pressed the gadget once again. His signal was answered. One of the Destroyers was close by. Crouched low, pistol held at the ready, he began to move through the undergrowth cautiously towards the sound. Suddenly he stopped short.

A still white face was staring at him from the bushes a matter of ten yards away!

'Who is it?' he hissed.

There was no reply.

'Is that you, Stevens?'

Still there was no answer.

Cautiously he crept closer. The figure did not move. The white blur of the face followed him without any sign of recognition. In a sudden gust of wind the man in the bushes moved and he saw that it was the body of one of the dead men from St Pancras, his shroudlines caught in a tree.

He lowered his pistol and breathed out a sigh of relief.

'It's that poor kid who roman-candled at Ringway,' a voice said in the shadows to his right. It was Stevens. 'Scared the life out of me too when I first saw him, sir,' he admitted, staring at the body swaying in the wind. 'I nearly wet me knickers and no kidding!'

'Where are the others?'

'The Yank and that Eyetie bloke are down beyond the glade here. I think I heard someone else a bit further off. The wind caught Thaelmann and Peters.'

'All right, let's start getting this thing on the road. We haven't much more time left before dawn.'

'You mean when the Jerries come looking for us!' Stevens said grimly, gripping his American-made 'grease gun' firmly and following Crooke.

'Yes, when the Jerries come looking for us,' Crooke echoed.

Together they disappeared into the darkness.

Phase Two of Operation Mincemeat was underway.

SECTION TWO:
THE TRAP

'But let me remind you that we're here on a military operation, not on a skylark in the Roman fleshpots!' *Lt. Crooke to the Destroyers*

CHAPTER ONE

The wind had dropped a little now, but it was still strong enough to move the body of the dead paratrooper hanging from the tree. The old soldier who had been killed in the pub brawl now lay on his back in the middle of a glade, his left arm and leg sprawled out with his right arm and leg tucked underneath his body oddly. A hundred yards away from him the *Oberleutnant*, his camouflaged para smock ripped down the front, was crumpled on his side like a rag doll which some child had thrown carelessly to one side.

'Sir,' Peters whispered, 'they're coming,' and pointed up the hill to their front. Faintly outlined against the skyline Crooke spotted a head and behind it what appeared to be a file of crouching men. Obviously some local peasant had spotted the drop and reported it to the authorities.

As the Destroyers took up their positions Crooke silently prayed that whoever had spotted them hadn't been able to count the number of parachutes.

He dropped to the ground at the edge of the firs and then worked his way in backwards as the Destroyers had done, closing the grass and undergrowth behind him. Drawing his revolver, he glanced quickly to left and right. Thaelmann was on his right and the Yank with Giggles to his left, hidden in a patch of gorse. If anything went wrong the enemy patrol would not live long enough to report their discovery.

Outlined now by the first rays of the sun, Crooke could see that there were six of them, led by an NCO who held a Schmeisser machine pistol in his arms and watched his front alertly, as if he expected trouble.

Suddenly one of the soldiers shouted, *'Herr Oberfeld. Hier drüben!'*

The soldier had discovered the leg pack which the Destroyers had carefully placed on the hillside so that any searcher would be drawn to the three dead men. The patrol doubled to the spot.

For what seemed like a long time, they crowded round it, obviously examining its contents. Then the NCO rapped out an order and they spread out again, advancing carefully, their weapons at the ready.

Suddenly the NCO in the lead stumbled and almost fell. *'Scheisse!'* he cursed and glared down at the object which had caused him to stumble. It was the *Oberleutnant's* body.

Tugging out his whistle, he blew it hard and placed his hand, fingers outstretched, on the crown of his helmet – the signal for 'rally me'.

The morning stillness was broken by their excited chatter. Crooke relaxed a little as Thaelmann crawled to his side and whispered an interpretation of their surprised comments.

Finally the NCO cut them short. 'All right,' he shouted as if he were on a parade ground. 'These are the ones that the old Macaroni reported to the captain. You,' he ordered the soldier who had found the second body, 'double back up the hill and get him and his cart!'

The soldier snapped to attention. *'Jawohl, Herr Oberfeld!'* The soldier slung his rifle over his shoulder and doubled away awkwardly up the hill.

The NCO turned to the other men and issued a stream of curt orders, which Thaelmann translated for Crooke. 'You search the bodies. You and you – over there on that knoll and keep your eyes skinned! There might be more of the Tommy bastards around. You and you – up there on the right! And do the same!' He watched them take up their positions, then unslinging his machine pistol he began to wander in Crooke's direction, his eyes obviously searching for further bits of paratroop equipment.

Thaelmann carefully cocked the big silenced Colt which he had picked from the OSS armoury for the operation. Slowly, supporting himself on one elbow, he brought up the pistol and took aim. The German sergeant kicked the grass idly with his boots, his eyes fixed on the ground. He was only ten yards away now and at any second he was bound to spot them. Then all hell would break loose.

Suddenly the NCO stopped. Crooke could see his face quite clearly now – brutal, powerful jaw, hard, stern eyes, toothbrush moustache. Instinctively he began to count the seconds as Thaelmann's finger curled round the trigger. In one more second the NCO would be dead and the whole operation would be a failure.

The squeak of rusty cart wheels cut into his consciousness. *'Herr Oberfeld,'* the man guarding the bodies shouted. *'Die Itaker sind da!'*

The NCO shouldered his Schmeisser and doubled back to the bodies. Crooke let out an audible sigh of relief and glanced quickly at Thaelmann. The German licked his lips and lowered the Colt.

'He'll never know, will he?' he said.

'What?'

'How close he came to dying.'

Crooke grinned. 'I suppose you're right. But it would be a good story to tell his kids after the war, wouldn't it?'

Thaelmann shrugged. 'If he lives to have any kids.'

While they watched, the NCO snapped at the ancient wrinkled peasant, 'All right, Macaroni, load the bodies. *Subito!'*

'Allora, signor capitano!' the old man said wearily, as if he had been used to taking orders like this all his life. Helped by one of the recruits he loaded the bodies on to the cart. Another soldier shinned up the tree bearing the dead paratrooper and began sawing away at the shroudlines with his bayonet. Eventually the body fell to the ground and the peasant trudged over and with the aid of the other soldier loaded it on the cart.

The NCO took a last look round the site but he could see nothing to keep him there any longer. 'All right, Macaroni,' he ordered in his bad Italian, 'move that race-horse of yours!'

With the unthinking cruelty of the Italian peasant, the old man pulled out his knife and dug it into the animal's skinny backside. With a rusty squeak, the cart began to move up the incline, the Germans, their weapons slung now, following.

Crooke waited until they had disappeared over the crest of the hill. Then he rose from his cover, followed by Thaelmann. 'All right, you can come out now,' he said, still keeping his voice low.

'Where's Yank?' Thaelmann asked.

'He's over there in the gorse!' Stevens raised his voice. 'Yank?'

There was no reply.

'Yank,' he called again.

Still no reply.

Gippo thrust his long knife into his belt and doubled over to the clump of gorse. He thrust his way into the prickly bush. 'Sir,' he called. 'Please be coming. It's the Yank. He's been knocked out and the other American gentleman – he is gone!'

CHAPTER TWO

'But where would the little bastard go?' Stevens asked as they crouched in the high grass around Crooke.

Crooke shook his head. 'Frankly, I don't know. All I know is that I wouldn't trust him as far as I could throw him. He's out to save his own skin in any damned way he knows how.'

'He'll shop us then, the bugger!' Stevens said.

Crooke nodded.

'We're in trouble,' Peters said, as he tried to clean the congealed blood from the wound in Yank's head.

The Texan raised himself on his elbow. 'That little dago would sell his own mother for a plugged nickel. As soon as he knew that we was watching those Krauts, he took his chance of bugging out.'

'Yer,' Stevens said thoughtfully, 'that's one thing. If he'd have wanted to shop us to the Jerries, why didn't he just shout out when they was here? That would have been the simplest way of getting us off his back.'

Crooke was deep in thought. He knew they didn't have much time left. If the Mafia man was going to betray them to the authorities, buying his own freedom with their lives, the police would be coming looking for them soon. But where were they to go, for without the Italian they were lost?

'I must admit we're in a bit of a fix. It's pretty obvious that he's going to use us to buy his own freedom. But it seems he was not prepared to do business with the Jerries. Perhaps,' he shrugged, 'he'll contact the Italian police. At all events, we can't hang around here much longer. Now I suggest we...'

'Sir, can I interrupt?' It was Thaelmann.

'What is it?'

'I know we haven't much time, sir. But perhaps we have a little more than you think.'

'What do you mean?'

'Well, sir, it's my guess that Giggles won't go to the Germans because he doesn't know them and he'll by-pass the police because of his past record. After all he's not the kind of man who would go to them voluntarily.'

'Well, where will he go then?'

'To the Ovra.'

'The what?'

For an answer Thaelmann pulled open the front of his thin civvies shirt. 'The Ovra,' he said and jabbed a thumb at the brown puckered letters on his chest. 'Burned into my skin on the night of 5 May, 1936, by a select crew of its members. I don't know much Italian but I know what those initials mean – *Organizzione Vigilanza Repressione Antifascismo.*' He let them stare at the brand for a moment and then buttoned up his shirt. 'In 1936 after I got out of Dachau, the German *KPD*★ smuggled me over the German border into Austria and from there the *apparat* got me down to the Southern Tyrol where I hid out with some German-speaking peasants and sympathisers near Bolzano. But someone must have talked. One night the bastards who did that,' he tapped his chest, 'came out to the farm to get me. They wanted to know who had helped me across the border and who my contacts were in Germany. I suppose they wanted to get in well with their friends of the Gestapo. When I wasn't prepared to sing, they gave me the old castor oil treatment first, but they were in a hurry and

★Illegal pre-war German Communist Party.

they wanted the information fast. Then they branded me. But the swine didn't get anything out of me. So they flung me in the barn and promised they were going to castrate me in the morning if I didn't talk. You know for the Italians with all their pride in their sexual ability, that's the ultimate threat.'

'What happened then?' Gippo prompted.

'I strangled the guard on the barn door and then I battered the other three to death with a shovel until there was nothing left of their faces.'

Gippo shuddered and swallowed hard. For a moment there was silence. The Destroyers lowered their eyes as if they were embarrassed by Thaelmann's confession.

'But what is Ovra?' Crooke said gently, breaking the silence.

'The Italian Gestapo, you could call it. In the early twenties, Mussolini tried to smash the Mafia. He succeeded in a way by simply enrolling the Sicilian Mafia into the Ovra and moving them to different parts of the country, as for example up to the Tyrol. It was their job to liquidate the opposition to the fascists – communists, socialists, liberals and the like. One of the first big leaders they killed was Matteotti, the head of the parliamentary opposition. But that was only the beginning. The Mafiosi began to use their old Sicilian methods – beatings, torture, murder, bribery. They all became the order of the day with Ovra. By the time Italy went into the war in 1940, the Ovra had become the country's regularly constituted secret police – the equivalent of Himmler's Gestapo. And the Ovra was being run by the ex-Mafiosi...' His voice trailed away, as if he had suddenly become aware that he was talking too much.

Stevens was the first to see the full implications of Thaelmann's revelation. 'So you think that Giggles would contact them and not the regular police force?' Thaelmann nodded. 'Because he'd be able to find mates in the Ovra or blokes who thought like he did – who wouldn't ask too many awkward questions, but would get on with the job and let him bugger off without any fuss?'

Again Thaelmann nodded.

'But where would he find the Ovra representatives?' Crooke asked.

'There are Ovra men in every town, sir. When I was in the Tyrol in hiding, the peasants told me that they thought one man in every ten in the big cities was an

Ovra agent.'

'So the best bet for him to find the Ovra is in Reggio itself?'

'Yes.'

'So what are we waiting for?' Yank said. 'Let's get the road to Reggio staked out. We'll bushwhack the bastards when they come looking for us.' He touched his sore head gingerly where the Italian had clubbed him with a rock. 'I'm looking forward to meeting up with that little dago again.'

The big black Fiat tourer was obviously the Ovra car. Its front was pretentious, heavy with chrome and a row of unnecessary head-lamps. But it wasn't the car's appearance which convinced the Destroyers, who had been waiting for hours in the heat of the dried-out ditch; it was the slowness with which the car crawled up the road from Reggio. Obviously its occupants were look-ing for the cart track which led to the spot where the Destroyers had been dropped.

'It's them, I'm sure,' Crooke whispered as the Destroyers peered through the thick cactus hedge. 'They're looking for us.'

When the car finally came to a halt at the turning the Destroyers cocked their weapons. An undersized Italian got out. In spite of the blazing afternoon heat he was dressed in a long, ankle-length coat with a broad-brimmed felt hat pulled well down over his forehead; he looked like a bit player in an old Hollywood gangster film. For a few moments he inspected the turn-off. Then he returned to the car and conferred with the other three occupants. From their hiding place the Destroyers could see the hand-waving and gesticulation.

Finally he got in again beside the driver, who backed into the middle of the road and edged the car round into the track with difficulty. In low gear the Fiat began to bump noisily up the track.

Crooke nudged Gippo. 'All right, Gippo. You'd better go into your act.'

Gippo picked up the blood-stained khaki handkerchief which had been used to bind Yank's head and wiped it on his face. When he was finished, he looked as if he had been involved in a serious accident.

'Stevens, you and Peters back up Gippo in case anything goes wrong. As soon as we've pulled it off, get the bodies out – sharpish!' Crooke turned to Yank. 'You'll stay with me. I need you in reserve,' he added, to appease the Texan, whose face bore a disgruntled look because he was being kept out of

81

action. Crooke looked at Thaelmann, who was watching the car intently. 'Well, it's up to you now. Remember though – no damage to the car. We need it.'

Thaelmann did not take his eyes off the vehicle. 'There is no need to tell me that, sir,' he said slowly. 'After what they did to me, I'm not going to waste good lead.' With his free hand he tapped the barrel significantly. 'I've got an old score to settle.' As Crooke had predicted the Fiat stopped with a lurch as it rounded the corner and the driver spotted Gippo lying flat on his face in the dust. A sallow-faced little man got out. Cautiously he approached Gippo, hand dug deep in the pocket of his big black overcoat, obviously clutching a pistol. For a moment he looked down at the inert body, then he placed his gleaming patent-leather shoe under him and heaved him over.

Gippo's blood-stained face and the hole in his forehead made with the aid of a cigarette end convinced him. '*Sta bene,*' he turned and began to tell the others. '*Il–*'

His sentence ended in a scream of pain as Gippo threw the knife he had hidden in his shabby jacket. It caught him in the middle of his chest. His mouth fell open and his legs began to buckle underneath him.

Horrified, the men inside the tourer stared at him. The driver grabbed for his pistol but it was the last thing he ever did. Thaelmann fired. There was a soft plop and he slumped forward on to the wheel. Behind him the man in the back fell to one side, a neat hole through his temple. Next to him his companion, a ratlike bald-headed man, tried to open the door and sneak out. Thaelmann fired again. Another soft plop. The bald-headed man flew through the open door, as if he had been kicked out by a horse. He was dead before he hit the dust.

In less than a minute it was all over. The big V-8 engine was still ticking over calmly. The hand brake was pulled tight. Three of the men were dead and the man Gippo had knifed was dying fast. Everything was perfect save for one thing – *Giggles was not in the car!*

Hurriedly, Crooke went over to the dying man, his hands still clutched weakly around the knife protruding from his chest. *'Dove e Cicconi?'* he asked in the best Italian he could muster.

The man's eyes opened. 'I speak American,' he said thickly. 'I live in Brooklyn once.'

'Well, where's Giggles?' Crooke said.

'Where is he?'

The Italian grinned feebly. 'On his way to Rome and the Duce...' Then his eyes rolled upwards, his mouth dropped open and his head fell to one side. He was dead.

CHAPTER THREE

Things happened quickly after that. They buried the bodies of the secret policemen in the ditch as best they could, having taken their passes from them. An hour later they had found the local German barracks and were just in time to spot a small convoy, escorted by an armoured car, leaving the main gate. Watching from the Fiat, which was parked in a side street, they saw the reason for the armoured car. As the big MAN truck, which brought up the rear of the little convoy, roared by, they caught a glimpse of a German NCO's face peering out of the back and behind him the mottled colours of an airborne smock.

'It's them,' Crooke whispered, 'and it looks as if they've found the documents. Thaelmann...'

But Thaelmann needed no orders. He put the car into gear and followed the German convoy at a discreet distance. It threaded its way through the crowded streets of Reggio until the armoured car in the lead turned on to the main road which led north.

'All right, pull over,' Crooke ordered, as the convoy disappeared northwards. Thaelmann did as he was told. Crooke got out of the seat next to him and said, 'Gippo, hop in here. You've got the Ovra pass and you speak a bit of Italian. Now this is the plan. We're not going to tail the convoy all the way to its destination. That is bound to arouse their suspicions. We're going to check it as it enters every major town on the way to Rome, which I guess is its destination, just to make sure that it is going to the capital. Then we'll be waiting for it on the outskirts of Rome.'

'But how will we manage when it gets dark, sir?' Peters asked. 'The Jerries'll only have their blue convoy lights. Not much to go by – and there's plenty of traffic about.' He indicated a group of German trucks passing by.

'Yes, but they're going south. Obviously they're building up their strength here, now that we've landed in Sicily. Besides we've got that armoured car to go by. I doubt if there'll be many armoured cars going north. Anyway, we've got to take that risk. Okay, Thaelmann, we're off to Rome.'

'The immoral city,' Stevens breathed.

'*Immortal,*' Thaelmann corrected him with Prussian precision.

Stevens grinned. 'I know what I'm talking about, mate. You have yer immortal, I'll have me immoral.'

They drove through the night, stopping at regular intervals to check whether the convoy was still on the road to Rome. Every time Crooke's guess proved right. The hours passed. Twice red lamps flashing in the darkness indicated a road block and check point. But Gippo's carelessly handed out Ovra pass worked wonders. The scruffy Italian guards, with their trailing puttees and down-at-heel shoes waved them on as if they were the devil himself. On and on. The big Fiat ate up the kilometres on the broad road north, empty save for the rumble of German Army trucks on the other side heading south towards the invasion front.

Towards dawn they started to come into the outskirts of Rome. The grey stone farmhouses began to give way to the white stucco villas of the rich Romans. Crooke ordered Peters, who had now taken Thaelmann's place at the wheel, to slow down. He yawned. It was nearly five o'clock. Beside him the others began to wake up. 'Okay,' he said, 'pull over in that side street there – where you can see that picture of Musso.' He indicated a ripped, fly-blown poster of the Duce, his great black jaw stuck out threateningly in that famous posture which Crooke remembered from the pre-war newsreels.

The Fiat pulled over. Stiffly, the Destroyers got out and stretched their legs. The city was still quiet. The streets were empty save for a few flea-ridden dogs sniffing the gutters for scraps. But in the food-short Rome of 1943, there were no scraps, even for them.

Slowly Crooke strolled to the communal water-tap, which like everything they had seen in Italy since they had landed was marked with a Roman bundle of rods, the symbol of the fascists. He turned on the tap, but only a trickle of water came out. It was symbolic of the new 'Roman Order'; it was a façade, behind which everything was decayed and useless. He bent and washed his face and hands, then cupping them to form a bowl drank the water. It tasted brackish. 'Okay,' he said when he got back to where the Destroyers lounged against a wall. 'They should be coming soon. When they do, we follow.' He turned to Stevens. 'You take over the wheel, Stevens. And woe betide you if you lose them.'

'Willdo, sir,' Stevens answered easily.

Slowly the suburb came to life. At the café across the way, an elderly waiter shuffled out in felt slippers, bellowed at one of the mangy dogs and began to take down the chairs piled on the tables outside. A couple of workmen in overalls pedalled slowly by, bottles of red wine stuck out of the cheap attaché cases fixed to their racks. They threw a curious glance at the men lounging against the wall; then they saw the big black Fiat and immediately they quickened their pace and drew away swiftly. Obviously, the car was immediately identifiable as belonging to the dreaded secret police.

Time passed. An ancient Model T Ford, made into a truck, rumbled over the cobbles, powered by the coal-gas trailer it towed behind it. It was piled high with vegetables for Rome's markets. Behind it came a one-legged veteran of one of Mussolini's ill-fated campaigns, clad in a dirty grey-green uniform, with his begging bowl already strapped to his waist. As he passed them, he hawked and spat deliberately at their feet.

'Cheeky bastard!' Stevens began, then stopped abruptly. There was the sound of powerful engines and the roar of some heavy vehicle changing down before taking the corner. Next moment the German armoured car swung into sight.

'It's them,' Crooke snapped, 'into the car.'

As Stevens swung behind the wheel and started the engine, the convoy, covered with dust, with blue lights still burning, sped past them. At a discreet distance they followed the last truck. They drove for about half an hour, straight through the centre of the capital, which was beginning to fill up with official cars, army trucks and mule-drawn farm carts. They crossed the Tiber and headed north along the river bank until the armoured car commander stood up in his turret and waved his red and white traffic disc to indicate that the convoy should turn off the main road. Finally, they drew up outside a great grey pile of a building, the windows of which were barred.

Stevens turned the Fiat in the opposite direction and pulled up in a dirty side street, lined with tumbledown eighteenth century houses, facing the building outside which the convoy had drawn up. Trying to appear as casual as possible, the Destroyers got out and, lounging against the wall of the nearest house, watched the activity across the road.

After a few minutes a little door at the side of the building opened and a man in German uniform checked the vehicles, then opened the main entrance and the truck containing the bodies entered. After some minutes it drove out again with the big NCO sitting in the cab next to the driver. Obviously he had delivered his load.

Crooke nodded to Gippo as the convoy started up again. 'Come on,' he ordered, 'let's go and have a shufti.'

Together they dodged the traffic which was already thickening considerably and crossed the street. Moments later they were back to tell the waiting Destroyers what they had discovered. 'It's a prison,' Crooke explained. 'The Regina Coeli Prison.'

'Yes, and there are Germans on guard at the side,' Gippo added. 'That must be their part of it.'

'What now, sir?' Peters asked softly. 'Have we to wait here till Admiral Canaris comes to have a look-see at the stiffs?'

Crooke shook his head. 'No, too damn dangerous. We've got to try to keep the prison under surveillance naturally. But we've got to get off the streets before someone starts asking awkward questions. I know we've got the Ovra passes, but if anyone begins to quiz us in Italian, we've had it.'

'What do you suggest, sir?' Thaelmann asked.

'That's a good question.' Crooke rubbed his jaw thoughtfully. 'We've got plenty of money, but we can't really go into the nearest hotel and ask for rooms.'

The Destroyers fell silent. Then Stevens said, 'Sir, I think I know a way out.'

'How?'

'Well, sir, I don't like to make promises, but if I can have Gippo with me and use the loot, I think I can pull it off. When you've been on the trot like I have and you've got no papers, there's only one way to get off the streets.'

'And that is?'

Stevens winked conspiratorially. 'Leave it to me and Gippo, sir.'

An hour later, during which the remaining Destroyers had waited with mounting concern, the two of them reappeared walking jauntily down the backstreet, their arms linked in those of a tall peroxided blonde whose great breasts threatened to burst through the tight red silk of her blouse at any moment.

'Oh, my holy Christ,' Yank breathed. 'Get a load of that broad! All that goddamn meat and no potatoes!'

Crooke sprang out of the car as they came level with it. 'What the devil are you up to?' he snarled.

Stevens was in no way put out. Neither was Gippo; his little black eyes gleamed lecherously and he licked his lips continually as he kept glancing at the blonde's voluptuous figure.

'Let me introduce you, sir. This is Irma.'

The big blonde beamed. Taking a deep breath so that her breasts again seemed to threaten to burst her blouse, she stuck out her hand. 'I'm glad to be seeing you,' she said in a pseudo-American accent. 'How are you going?'

The Yank shook his head. 'Willya look at them lungs on her!'

Crooke reddened with embarrassment. 'Who is she?' he stuttered, pulling back his hand, as if her grasp were red-hot.

'I thought you'd guess, sir,' Stevens said. 'When you're on the trot, there's only one way to get off the street if you ain't got papers – you find a knocking shop.'

'A what?'

'A brothel, sir,' Peters explained gently. 'That's what the men call it.'

'*Si, si,*' the big blonde agreed eagerly, her breasts trembling beneath the shimmering red silk, as if they had an independent existence, '*bordello.*'

'Hot shit,' the Yank said enthusiastically, 'we're gonna go into a dago whorehouse!'

The girl beamed and hugged Gippo to her delightedly. Crooke clapped his hand to his forehead and said weakly, 'All right, Stevens, get her in the car. But if you've made a ballsup of this one, God help you!'

CHAPTER FOUR

Irma opened the door to the back of the delicatessen which graced the ground floor of the big ramshackle house in which what she called 'my establishment' was located. She touched her finger to her bright-red lips conspiratorially. With exaggerated care, she tip-toed in, followed by the Destroyers.

93

Silently, they threaded their way through shelves of stale-smelling salamis and trays of potato salad in ersatz mayonnaise, whose yellow edges had gone crusty and dry. 'Black market,' she commented. 'All black market today.' In passing she dipped her finger into the mayonnaise and licked it appreciatively. 'Good, eh. You try.' But none of the Destroyers were tempted to follow her example. 'Get the trots from that,' Yank said sourly, 'even without touching it.'

Irma opened the door which led to her 'establishment' and waited till they were all collected at the foot of the stairs. She opened the door at the head of the steep rickety stairs and led them into a dark dusty corridor, heavy with the smell of food and ancient lecheries. There she threw open another door to reveal a large room, filled with shabby, overstuffed red plush furniture and yellowing pictures which revealed immediately what the room's purpose was. *'Allora* – the salon!' she announced proudly.

For a moment she allowed them to take in the place, as if it were worthy of serious study. Then she clapped her hands. 'And now my girls,' she said with the Italian sense of the dramatic.

A hard-faced ageing blonde appeared

from the nearest door, stifling a yawn. She was wearing high-heeled boots, laced to the knee in the fashion of the late nineteenth century. Her fat body was forced into a tight black shining satin corset, which attempted to hold up her sagging breasts and failed lamentably.

'*Tu Irma!*' she said lazily and yawned out-loud, not attempting to cover her mouth, filled with gold teeth.

'Renate,' the brothel-owner explained. 'Before the war she was belonging to an English milord. A great gentleman, but old.' She winked. 'You understand – old and in need of energetic treatment. Now she is for special gentlemen.' As if to emphasise the point, Renate cracked the switch she was carrying against the side of her black boot. But she did so without any force, her plump broad face blank of any emotion save boredom and tiredness.

Another door opened. A younger woman, with dark loose hair falling to her shoulders and framing her deathly pale face, peered round it. She was fully dressed save for shoes. Her black stockings were darned and there was a button missing from the waist of her skirt.

'Rachele,' Irma introduced her.

'*Giorno*,' the girl whispered hoarsely and then coughed.

Irma put her arm round the woman's thin shoulders and escorted her to the sagging couch. 'The war,' she said over her shoulder. 'Damn war. No money – no food.' She turned her attention to the girl who was undergoing a fit of thick coughing and muttered something to her soothingly in her native tongue.

Crooke took the opportunity to speak to Stevens. 'Okay, what's the deal?'

'Simple, sir. I have made a deal with her. For the money I had she's prepared to put us up and close the place for the next few days. I told her we was Yankee aircrew who had escaped from a Eyetie POW camp. She has a soft spot for the Yanks – her brother moved there in the twenties. And of course the dough helped. Anyhow she bought it.'

'And what else?'

'What do you mean, sir?'

'Come off it, Stevens. You know bloody well what I mean! Those women! What's the deal with them?'

The cockney looked down at his shabby Italian shoes. 'Well, sir,' he began hesitantly, 'it's hard to explain.'

Gippo who had obviously misunderstood

Crooke's look butted in hastily. 'Oh yes, sir. Everything is okay. The price is including the jig-jig with the girls. The beautiful Irma, she is promising me first go. But if you are wishing it, you may have my turn.'

'Oh shut up,' Crooke snapped. 'All right, Stevens, I buy the idea. I have no alternative. But let me remind you we're here on a military operation, not on a skylark in the Roman fleshpots. And you're soldiers under orders. That said, let's get down to business. First get those damn women out of here.'

After the women had been shooed out, a little puzzled and angry that their ageing charms were not required, Crooke turned to the Destroyers whose eyes were fixed on the fly-blown drawings of intricate copulations on the walls. 'All right, pay attention to me, will you! Now, we're going to put a round-the-clock watch on that prison – at least during daylight hours. Two of us at a time from eight till it gets dark.'

'What exactly are we looking for, sir?' Peters asked.

'The Admiral in charge of the German *Abwehr* – Canaris. We've got to find out whether he comes to view the bodies. If we know that, we know that the plan is beginning to work. At least – that the news has got to the top. Whether he'll be fooled by the documents they're carrying or not – that's something else.'

'But how will we recognise this Admiral?' Yank asked.

Crooke sketched in what he knew of the *Abwehr* chief's background – his career as a naval officer and spymaster who was reputed to have been the lover of Mata Hari in World War One; his slow rise as chief of Hitler's Intelligence; and his association with those military leaders in Germany's hierarchy who had now begun to oppose the Führer. 'As far as I know there is nothing outstanding about his appearance. He's average height, has a wrinkled, sallow face and white hair so that he looks older than he really is. He could be wearing naval uniform, but according to Commander Mallory, our people in Berlin say that he's gone off uniforms over these last years. He prefers civvies.'

'Not very much to go on,' Thaelmann remarked.

'Agreed. But there is one certain way of recognising him. The Admiral's crazy about dogs. A couple of times our people in Spain have picked up top secret messages to Berlin when he's been there, asking about the welfare of his pooches. This time, however, he'll have them with him. So,' he concluded, 'if you spot an elderly pleasant-looking gent leading a couple of dachshunds, you'll know it's our man.'

They spotted him on the afternoon of the next day. In spite of the heat, the pavements on both sides of the road in front of the prison were crowded, for which Crooke, accompanied by Gippo, was grateful; the crowd provided excellent cover.

'Looks like a parade, Gippo,' he whispered as they stood back and watched Blackshirt militiamen and policemen, wearing blue uniforms and bearing huge swords, trying to force the spectators back off the road.

Up the street there came a faint burst of cheering, but it was without enthusiasm. Moments later a drum major came into view, his chest thrust out, leading the military band in the Roman goose-step borrowed from Germany after Mussolini had paid a visit to Hitler before the war. Behind came the ranks of boys in the fascist *Balilla* movement, taking themselves very seriously as they marched by, carrying their dummy wooden rifles. But if the boys and the 'Sons of the Wolf' who followed them took themselves seriously, Crooke could see that the crowd was not impressed. All around him their faces were filled, not with martial pride at these bellicose sons of Italy, but with sorrow that soon the smooth-faced youths would be cannon fodder in one or other of Mussolini's ill-fated armies. The parade dragged on. Band followed band, with the boys giving way to the white-clad girls of the *Piccole Italiane* and *Giovani Italiane*, the fascist girl organizations.

Suddenly, a cavalcade of sleek black Mercedes came racing up the opposite side of the road, horns sounding shrilly. The leading car, an open tourer filled with black-clad SS men, with troopers hanging on both doors, did not slow down when it came abreast of the parade. Instead the driver pressed the horn with all his strength. The drum major faltered. His baton came down and clattered to the cobbles and the next moment the band scattered wildly. Behind them the girls screamed and broke ranks. In an instant the whole parade was a confused mess of screaming, frightened, angry shouting Italians.

The Mercedes braked to a halt. The black giants dropped from the sides and lined up superciliously, their hands on their revolver belts, staring into nothing, not deigning to notice the crowd of Italians around them.

A high ranking SS officer stepped out. He turned and opened the door of the car behind him. Courteously he helped its white-haired occupant out. Two dachshunds followed yelping at his feet.

'*Canaris!*' Crooke said quickly.

'Is it?'

'Yes, no mistaking him,' Crooke said.

In tense silence they waited until the procession of high-ranking German *Abwehr* and SS police officers had disappeared inside the Regina Coeli Prison. Then they decided it was time to go. All around them the crowd was muttering sullenly about the way the Germans had ruined the parade – and Crooke did not want any trouble. He decided that they'd better make themselves scarce and in his haste to get away, he failed to spot the skinny little man who had been staring at them intently for the last ten minutes. Now as the two Destroyers pushed their way through the crowd, he put the two silver half dollars with which he had been playing back in his pocket and began to follow them.

CHAPTER FIVE

The SS came just before dawn. A whistle shrilled and in the cobbled street heavy boots clattered towards the brothel. A harsh voice bellowed an order and there was a vicious hammering on the door of Irma's establishment.

Crooke woke with a start. Outside it was still fairly dark. For a moment he struggled to wake up. Then, flinging himself out of bed, he grabbed his clothes and pistol and sprang to the window. Big trucks were pulled up on the other side of the road and heavily armed SS troopers in coal-scuttle helmets were pouring out of them to surround the house. They were trapped!

The hammering at the door became ever more insistent as he pulled on his clothes, and dashed into the corridor. Stevens was standing there, completely naked, his American machine pistol clutched across his white chest, facing the door. The SS were using axes now. Gippo came out of the same room. He was naked too. Behind him

Irma, her face deathly pale, was frantically trying to get into her flowered kimono; her hands trembled violently.

Then the door gave way and the SS trooper who had been using the axe stumbled in. But his cry of triumph ended in a strangled scream as Stevens pressed the trigger of the grease gun. The volley caught him full in the face at short range. Stevens fired again. Behind the dying SS man another man was flung backwards. Then the machine pistol jammed. A third SS trooper raised his pistol as Stevens frantically tried to clear the stoppage.

The SS man pushed aside the body in front of him but at the same moment a knife flew through the air and caught the SS man in the throat. He went down screaming. Behind him the rest fled the way they had come.

Now the hall was filling up with the rest of the Destroyers, weapons in their hands. The two other women appeared, Renate naked save for her high black boots, and her whip which she held firmly, as if prepared to drive off the Germans single-handed. *'Chi e–'* she began in her husky voice.

A high-pitched burr of machine-gun fire drowned her words. Slugs ripped along the whole length of the brothel. Windows shattered and broken glass and plaster came tumbling down. 'My house,' Irma screamed, 'my poor beautiful house–'

'Get your head down,' Crooke bellowed and pushed her down to the floor. 'All of you down!'

They needed no urging. A searchlight had been flicked on below. As the spandau continued to fire, it swung along the front of the building trying to find them. 'You should better surrender,' a harsh voice commanded over a loud hailer. 'We have you surrounded. There is no escape for you!'

'Aw, go and crap in yer hat!' the Yank bellowed. Ignoring the stream of bullets which were tearing the ceiling and walls apart, he crawled towards the shattered door. With a grunt, he pushed the dead SS man over and grabbed the stick grenade thrust into his belt. He scuttled back up the corridor and into the kitchen, ducking under the beam of the searchlight. For an instant he raised himself and peered through the shattered window.

'There's one of them!' someone shouted in German.

But before the machine-gunner could swing his spandau round, Yank had pulled out the pin and flung the potato-masher through the window. 'Bite on that one, you bastards,' he yelled and scuttled back to safety as bullets hissed into the kitchen, sending the pots and pans flying to the floor.

'*Achtung!*' a voice shouted.

But before the Germans could take cover, the grenade exploded in their midst. Next moment the searchlight went out and the machine gun stopped firing. But not for long. The SS men retreated to the cover of their trucks and opened up again with increased fury. A prolonged burst of firing ripped through the brothel. As they pressed themselves to the wall of the corridor, with the bullets systematically shattering everything above waist level, Crooke realised that they would have to give in – or get out soon. Above him a framed poster showing the Italian liner *Roma* ploughing through a bright blue sea took a burst. The glass shattered into a thousand pieces.

'We've got to get out of here,' Crooke shouted.

'What about the backyard, sir?' Stevens cried.

'No good,' Thaelmann answered. 'They're out there waiting too.'

'The roof, sir?' Peters suggested.

'No good. Too steep. We're sitting ducks out there from both sides.'

'I know a way, *Signor Tenente,*' Irma said. Her fear had been overcome by anger at the destruction of her establishment. Now she was prepared to act. 'Follow me,' she ordered.

In a long file they crawled after her through the shattered debris of the corridor. Bringing up the rear with Renate, still clad only in her high black boots, Yank raised himself and fired a last burst through the window. 'That'll learn yer to keep yer goddamn heads down!' he cried and crawled rapidly after the rest.

Irma stopped at a little door. 'A way for gentlemen who are not wanting to be seen,' she explained. 'We use it now.' She smiled triumphantly. 'We fool the *tedeschi* yet.'

'Where does it lead to?' Crooke asked.

She wagged her finger at him. 'You will see – soon,' she said, her sense of the dramatic reasserting itself.

She opened it and they followed her swiftly up the narrow rickety stairs, which were pitch black. Once Yank bumped into Renate's backside as the woman missed her step and cried, 'Willya take yer ass outa my face!' But otherwise they negotiated them without difficulty. The noise of the firing from outside was somewhat subdued now.

Moments later they emerged into a dark loft.

'Keep your head under,' Irma ordered. 'The wood,' she meant the rough beams, 'is low.'

With Irma in the lead they ran along the length of the loft. Below the chatter of the machine guns had given way to the crackle of rifle fire. Soon, Crooke knew, the Germans would tumble to the fact that they had made a bolt for it and would come looking for them. Then they would rush the house.

Irma stopped suddenly. They had come up against a blank wall. 'What's the matter, missus?' Stevens asked. 'Where's the way out?' Irma swept her hand towards a large wardrobe standing against the wall.

'That cupboard. Open the door, please.'

Stevens did as she ordered, revealing that there was no back to the wardrobe. Behind he could see the vague outlines of another loft similar to the one they were in. They pushed through hurriedly.

Below the sound of firing had stopped altogether. The Germans would already be moving in. As they raced through the gloomy loft, Crooke reckoned to himself that they might have a chance after all. The Germans must be at least one hundred yards away. If they hadn't surrounded the whole quarter, they might yet get away with it.

Irma came to a halt. 'Now silence,' she gasped. She held up her finger to her lips. 'We are coming down the backstairs; they go to another street; but please, you are making no noise.' She fumbled in her pocket and pulled out a small rusty key. Carefully, she fitted it in the lock of the door which barred their way. It turned easily, as if it were regularly oiled. Crooke guessed that this was the way out for Renate's 'gentlemen with special tastes'. Hastily he pushed Irma to one side. 'Let me go first,' he whispered. He pulled out his pistol, gripped the door handle, and opened the door slowly.

'Okay, let's go,' he said softly. 'But look out.' Gripping his pistol more firmly, he passed through. A dark shape detached itself from the gloom. 'Mr Crooke, I think,' was the last thing the one-eyed officer heard as the heavy weight came crashing down on the back of his head.

CHAPTER SIX

'My name's Kappler – *Obersturmbannführer* Herbert Kappler,' the German standing at the door of their cell announced, as he stared down at them lying in the dirty straw. 'I am the police attaché at the German Embassy in Rome. I have been given charge of your case. But...' He turned abruptly and made way for the little man in civilian clothes behind him.

The white-haired civilian nodded his thanks gravely as Kappler said to the Destroyers, 'Perhaps you would be so kind as to stand up for the Admiral.' The Destroyers, still groggy and sore from the beating they had received at the hands of the SS men that morning, got to their feet slowly and stared at the little civilian.

'*Heil Hitler*,' he said without any enthusiasm, flapping up a soft hand momentarily, as if he knew it was something which was expected of him, but which bored him beyond measure. 'My name is Canaris. I am sure you will have heard of me.' He smiled softly and gave a queer, old-fashioned bow. 'I have been looking forward to meeting you,' he said in his stilted English, 'ever since we became aware of you in the desert last year. My young friend Baron von Foelkersam has told me a great deal about you. You have caused me much trouble.'

For a moment he studied their faces, while they stared back at him with a mixture of defiance and curiosity.

'Of course we now know how your clever young gentlemen of Naval Intelligence fooled us on Sicily. Major William Martin – what an excellent idea! It is a pity that Germany does not produce that kind of deviousness. I am afraid we Germans are a plain straightforward people. However, we know now that your little plan was intended to dupe us. The Italian gangster.' He clicked his manicured fingers at Kappler without looking round. 'What was his name?'

'Cicconi, *Exzellenz*,' Kappler said, clicking his polished boots together.

'Yes. Thank you. Well, your Cicconi has told us everything. We know all, you see.'

'The wop bastard!' the Yank snarled. 'I hope he fries in hell!'

Canaris looked at the Yank's battered face almost sadly. 'My friend you have learned a lesson from this episode – that you cannot place your trust in the human animal. That is why I love my dogs so much.' He sighed. 'Unfortunately you have learned it too late.'

'What do you mean – *sir?*' Crooke asked, adding the 'sir' because in some strange way he was impressed by the Admiral.

'I think I shall leave the unpleasant task of explaining that to *Obersturmbannführer* Kappler,' he answered. 'I just wanted to see you.' He turned to the SS police chief. Kappler clicked his heels together and rattled on the bars of their cell. The guards came and unlocked it from the outside and the SS officer opened the door for the Admiral with a flourish. *'Exzellenz,'* he snapped.

Canaris nodded his thanks gravely. He turned slowly and looked at them once more, his dark eyes as veiled and impenetrable as ever. 'Ours is a nasty business – a very nasty one,' he said. He touched his hand to his white hair, as if in greeting and said, 'Goodbye gentlemen. I am glad to have met you.'

Kappler waited till he had gone and the guard had locked the door again. Then he turned to them again, taking out a crumpled packet of cigarettes. *'Juno Eckstein,'* he said, 'not the best, but better than those Italian "V" things.' He handed over the packet. Those of the Destroyers who smoked lit up gratefully; they had had nothing to smoke since their capture that morning. Patiently he waited until they had done so. 'You will be wondering what the good Admiral meant?' he said.

Crooke nodded although he knew exactly what the Admiral had meant.

'Then let me explain. You were in civilian clothes and armed when arrested. You killed several of our soldiers at the same time, incidentally. Nor is this your first time behind our lines. You have previously been engaged on sabotage operations in both Germany and Russia. In short we could sentence you all to death as spies without the slightest problem. No civilised country in the western world would hesitate to do the same.'

'And in uncivilised ones such as yours, it would go even quicker,' Thaelmann sneered.

Kappler ignored this remark. 'Italy is crumbling fast. It is like a vast beautiful palace with,' he sought for the right word, 'a breathtaking façade; yet it is riddled with termites. One little tap with a child's hammer and it will all crumble into dust.

Such a place is Italy in 1943.'

'Very neatly put,' Crooke said looking up at the immaculate SS officer from the straw-covered floor. 'But what's that got to do with us, if you're going to kill us?'

Kappler looked down at him. 'You could help us to maintain that façade a little longer – at the price of your own and your men's lives. The Mussolini regime cannot stand another blow like yesterday's push from the beaches in Sicily and the retreat of the Italian Army. The man in the street is now not only anti-German, but also anti-Duce. And there are powerful men around the King and the Crown Prince who would be only too glad to see the Duce go, in spite of the fact that they owe him everything. With the Duce gone, Italy would be out of the war within the month. The Italians have no stomach for fighting any more. It is obvious that as soon as your troops have cleared up Sicily – and they will do so soon – they will invade the mainland of Italy. Your abortive mission has shown that. Now when you Tommies land – or the *Amis* for that matter – it would be a great boost for Italian prestige if they were to be thrown back into the sea by the Italian Army.' He smiled cynically. 'Naturally with a little aid from the *Wehrmacht!* And the Italians might well be able to do just that if they knew the exact spot where you are going to land.'

'And what concern of ours is this propaganda plan of yours?' Crooke asked, knowing the answer already.

'I think you know, Mr Crooke. You are an intelligent man. If, for instance, you would tell exactly where the First British Airborne Division is to drop, we might be tempted to forget your previous crime against the Third Reich – as well as the present abortive operation.'

Crooke opened his mouth to protest, but the SS officer held up his hand for silence. 'Perhaps you would prefer time to discuss the matter with your men. After all it's *their* lives too – not just that of yourself, officer and gentleman as you are. A Colonel Helfferich of Admiral Canaris' staff will be arriving here in exactly one hour. That should give you sufficient time. You can tell him.'

'And if we don't speak out?' Crooke said. 'What then?'

Kappler smiled pleasantly. He raised his long forefinger and pointed it at Crooke like a weapon; then he clicked the finger back and forth a couple of times as if he were pulling a trigger. And with that he was gone.

Punctually one hour later, Colonel Helf-ferich, a brisk middle-aged officer in *Wehrmacht* summer uniform, was ushered into their cell. He got down to business at once. His English was not as good as that of Kappler or of Canaris, but he made his point clearly enough.

'Which is you is the officer?' he asked.

'I am,' Crooke answered.

Helfferich looked at his battered face, with the great hole where the SS men had torn away his patch, and sniffed in disdain. 'Good. Then what have you decided?'

'We cannot betray our men – even if we knew where they were to drop,' Crooke said.

Helfferich accepted the information calmly. 'I see.' Turning to the others, he said, 'And what have you men decided?'

The Yank made a rude sound with his lips. 'The Bronx cheer to you, buddy,' he said.

'Good, then you have made your decision.' The Colonel walked to the cell door and rattled on the bars. 'Tell Carlo to bring me my briefcase,' he ordered.

A few moments later, the door was opened and a wave of perfume swept into the cell. An unbelievably handsome young Italian in

115

a tight-fitting chauffeur's uniform came tripping into the cell, the briefcase held out like a gift in his white, well-cared-for hands.

'Your case, Colonel,' he said in poor German. While Colonel Helfferich fumbled with a catch, he looked over at the Destroyers and, patting his carefully oiled hair, pursed his lips at them.

'Oh my holy Christ!' Stevens said, 'he's one of the boys! Navy cake, as sure as cats has kittens. Isn't he lovely?'

Suddenly the simpering look vanished from the chauffeur's face and he winked at them. But there was none of the usual homosexual affectation about the gesture.

Colonel Helfferich finally got the case open and looked up. 'Carlo, where are my glasses?'

'Here, sir,' the Italian said softly, one hand on his hip again. He placed the steel-rimmed spectacles in the Colonel's hand gently, almost lovingly.

'Thank you, Carlo,' the German officer said, putting them on and looking down at the sheet of paper he had taken out of the case. He cleared his throat and with his voice raised formally, he began to read. 'The Führer has confirmed the sentences of death passed on following prisoners – for sabotage and high treason in the case of Thaelmann and espionage in the case of all.' He rattled off their names, while they listened numbly, their attention directed at the homosexual chauffeur, whose sudden wink had seemed to be a sign of hope. Now, however, posing behind his boss, he did not seem to be concerned with them in the least.

The German officer raised his head and pronounced the sentence without the aid of the paper. 'You will be executed on Monday, 26 July, 1943, by firing squad.' He put the paper away in the case, closed it and took off his spectacles.

'Have you anything to say?'

They shook their heads in silence.

'Na schön.' He turned, picked up his cap and rattled on the bars for the guard, while the Destroyers stared at the chauffeur who was fussing with his hair again. Then, as the guard opened the door, something fell from his hand and dropped on to the floor. A moment later the two men were gone and the Destroyers were examining the object he had let fall.

Crooke turned it over. 'It's just an ordinary playing card,' he said slowly.

'Goddamn queer,' Yank said. 'It fits him,

don't it?'

'What do you mean?'

'Well, it's the Queen of Hearts – and Jesus he was a queen if I ever saw one.'

'Oh, crikey!' Stevens exclaimed and then his mouth dropped open stupidly.

'What's up?' the others cried.

'The Queen,' he said. 'That'd be too sodding good to be true! You remember when that Yank major briefed us in Algiers? Well, didn't he say that he had a source of information in Rome, who was a chauffeur or something like that? And do you lot remember the bloke's code name?'

'The Fairy Queen,' Thaelmann breathed.

'That's right,' Stevens said triumphantly. 'And I think we've just met his nibs.'

CHAPTER SEVEN

The Italian guard had just handed them their evening meal of a cup of sour red wine and a slice of stale bread covered with ersatz cheese paste when the riot started.

The door had hardly closed behind him when from down the long stone corridor

118

they heard the clash of metal against metal.

'What's that?' Crooke asked listlessly and put down his slice of bread.

'Sounds like somebody banging his mug against the bars,' Stevens said.

'Yeah, some poor bastard's gone stir-crazy,' said Yank. 'Who wouldn't in this goddamn dump?'

But the noise persisted, growing louder by the second. Soon the whole pile rocked with the ear-splitting noise of hundreds of men beating their cups against anything metal. Then the whistles began to blow. There was the clatter of heavy jackboots down the stone corridor. Orders were rapped out in Italian and German. Cell doors were flung open. But still the clamour continued, growing louder and louder by the minute.

Suddenly in the Destroyers' cell the electric light bulb flicked on, although it was not yet dark. Then it went off, then on again and this time stayed on a little longer before it flicked out once more. They stared at each other in bewilderment. 'What the sodding hell is going on?' Stevens said. The light was now going off and on at regular intervals, while outside the guards were mercilessly beating some unfortunate prisoner. They could hear the swish and thud of their

119

rubber clubs and the man's screams, all joining in the ever-increasing noise.

Suddenly Stevens, always quicker off the mark than the rest of the Destroyers, tumbled to it. 'It's morse,' he cried. *'Morse code!'*

'Can any of you read morse?' Crooke asked.

'Me, sir.' It was Peters.

'Good. Get to it!'

And soon Peters was spelling out the letters. 'U-S-S-O.'

'We've got the tail end of the message,' Crooke said. 'It must mean "Musso" –Mussolini.'

Peters was spelling out the next bit. 'D-E-E-D.' He blinked and looked away from the light. 'Deed?' he asked.

'Dead!' Stevens said. 'The bloke can't spell.'

From outside they heard a scream, high-pitched and hysterical, which ended in broken-hearted sobbing. But the row continued. Suddenly a voice rapped out an order in German. A single rifle shot rang out. Something heavy fell to the floor. A volley of shots echoed down the corridor, but when they died away, the clamour was still going on.

Then the bulb came on again and the same message was repeated. 'M-U-S-S-O … D-E-E-D.' But this time it was followed by something which made their hearts beat with new hope and determination. 'A-T-T-E-N-D … F-Q.'

'*The Fairy Queen!*' Stevens yelled exuberantly. '*It's him, sir!*'

The Destroyers broke into excited chatter. The little homosexual was up to something. Perhaps, after all, they would not be taken out next morning and placed against the bullet-pocked wall to undergo the ultimate military ritual!

'All right, lads,' Crooke said. 'It looks as if we've got a chance after all. There's something going on out there. Our little pansy's obviously going to use it to get us out. Let's be waiting for him.'

Yank grabbed a tin mug and banged it down hard on the bench, testing its suitability as a weapon. 'I'm ready to go.'

Outside the firing continued. But the noise persisted. The Italians and the SS men were hopelessly outnumbered; that was obvious. As soon as they quelled one area of noise, another broke out elsewhere. They heard the rattle of keys outside and Crooke nodded to Yank, who darted to the door, tin mug held aggressively in his fist. The door swung open. A bareheaded, bleeding militiaman stood there. Behind him, resplendent in the uniform of a colonel in the *carbinieri*, big pistol in his elegant hand, stood the Fairy Queen. 'My name is Colonel Piccoli,' he said severely, but the uniform and the voice could not quite hide his affected pose. 'I am to take you to the Podgora *carbinieri* Barracks for immediate execution. Come.' He waved the pistol at them.

Obediently they filed forward, trying to hide the grins on their faces at the Fairy Queen's martial transformation.

'You,' he said to the bleeding guard in Italian. 'Come with me. If they attempt to escape, shoot! You understand?'

'*Si, si*,' the other man said, only too glad to get out of the prison.

With the militiaman in the rear, holding his machine pistol, and the Fairy Queen in the lead, the Destroyers marched up the corridor, littered now with debris. As they passed an open cell, they saw a man lying in a pool of blood on the floor. The guards had smashed the back of his head in with his three-legged stool. Up ahead there was a sudden burst of firing, but the Fairy Queen did not hesitate. 'Come on – don't stop!'

An SS man was standing in the gloom at the end of the corridor, firing short sharp bursts from his *Schmeisser* at something high above his head. Scream after scream rang out. But he continued to fire. Suddenly he swung round and saw them. 'What do you want, Macaroni?' he said suspiciously in German, levelling his smoking machine pistol at them.

The Fairy Queen continued to smile pleasantly but kept moving forward. Whether he had understood or not, the Destroyers did not know. He fumbled in his pocket, as if he were looking for a pass. '*Ausweis,*' he said in German.

The SS man lowered his eyes for a moment instinctively and regretted it the next. The Fairy Queen's neat-booted foot shot up in the style of a Siamese foot boxer and crashed into the SS man's mouth. His helmet clattered to the floor and his head cracked backwards. With a stifled scream he flew backwards, hands groping towards his shattered face.

'Get him, Yank!' Crooke yelled.

The American swung round and hit the militiaman hard in the mouth. The pistol went flying and his head came forward to meet his hands but instead his chin found itself in abrupt contact with Yank's sharply rising knee. There was a dry snap like twigs underfoot. The militiaman rolled over, his spine broken.

Crooke thrust out his hand. 'Crooke – delighted to see you.'

The Fairy Queen grinned. 'Me too. But come. We have much to do!'

Crooke grabbed the SS man's machine pistol and Yank the militiaman's. They stepped over the bodies and hurried on.

'This way.' The Fairy Queen indicated a narrow door almost hidden in the gloom of the corridor. 'Watch me, please.'

As the Destroyers huddled there, Crooke and Yank turned outwards to cover the corridor, the Italian rapped on the door. It swung open to reveal a bald-headed fat man in the uniform of a captain in the militia.

'Hurry,' he said in English and held out a pasty white hand.

The Fairy Queen reached in his pocket and pulled out a small bag. There was the chink of coins. 'Two hundred – in gold sovereigns,' he said. 'Count them if you like.'

'I trust you,' the captain said. 'And there is no time. The prison is crazy. The Tedeschi will start massacring the prisoners at any moment.'

As if to emphasise his words, there was a prolonged burst of heavy machine gunfire from somewhere in the prison.

The captain flung up his hands in the expressive Latin fashion. 'Ah, now there we have it!'

The Fairy Queen pushed past him. 'Hurry,' he said. 'The car is in the courtyard. The guards on the gate are bribed. If the Germans don't get there first!'

As they ran across the courtyard, the sound of firing intensified behind them. A slug whizzed past them and splattered against the wall. Another ricocheted off the cobbles in a shower of sparks a few feet in front of them.

'Keep running!' Crooke bellowed.

They flung themselves into the waiting Asturia, the Fairy Queen behind the wheel. The car roared forward and with a squeal of rubber took the narrow corner. The main exit gate loomed ahead in the gloom. The Fairy Queen put his foot down hard on the accelerator. A group of bareheaded SS men came running out of a door. The Fairy Queen put his hand on the horn. Its blast swept them to one side in a mad scramble for safety. A machine pistol started firing behind them. Lead pattered against the back of the car. Ahead of them the militia scattered. But the gate was open. The bribe had worked.

The Asturia shot through. With an angry squeal of rubber, they took the corner beyond. Crouched deep in the big leather seat, the Fairy Queen swung the car into the main street. They were free!

'Where are we going?' Crooke shouted.

The Fairy Queen grinned. 'To see the Pope!' he yelled back.

Rome had gone crazy. As the news of Mussolini's downfall (for as the Fairy Queen told them, he had been mistaken – Mussolini was not dead, but deposed) spread, the people went wild.

The streets were suddenly filled with men and women dressed in nightgowns and pyjamas, the doors of their apartments flung wide open, the blackout regulations forgotten completely. Everywhere screaming mobs were wrecking the offices of the party. They passed the great Hotel Majestic. A mob of men came rushing out, bearing a beautiful film actress clad in yellow silk pyjamas, crying for some reason, known only to themselves. *Evviva il Re! Evviva il Papa!*

The Destroyers had never seen anything like it. 'Bloody hell, it's like the night the Aussies went crazy in Cairo's red light district in forty-two!' Stevens breathed, as they drove by a Party office where the mob was tumbling bronze Duce busts over a balcony and indulging in an orgy of destruction, scattering the square below with Party books, badges and torn bits of uniform.

They headed towards the Piazza Colonna, where they had to slow down while a big-bald-headed man, stripped to the waist and covered with sweat was dragging a bronze head of the Duce behind him with a rope.

Gradually they drew nearer the Vatican City. They passed a mob of long-haired young men, wearing red communist sashes, who were beating to death an elderly man dressed in the uniform of the Blackshirts. The Fairy Queen flipped his free hand at them. 'The sons of the Duce's Romans,' he said cynically. 'The wolves of Tuscany – beating an old man to death! Real men – eh?'

As they turned a corner they saw before them the main entrance to the Vatican City and beyond it the dome of St Peter's.

A mixed group of soldiers and armed

civilians rushed towards them, shouting. The Fairy Queen put down his foot. The mob parted, but one man was too late. The bonnet hit him squarely in the stomach. The Asturia lurched momentarily. Then the man fell from the bonnet and the wheels crunched over his dead body. They were through the entrance and into the sudden stillness of the Vatican.

Father O'Leary ushered them into an ancient waiting room that smelled of floor polish and official righteousness. 'The Monseigneur will see you now,' he said softly in an Irish accent. He rubbed his soft wet palms that hadn't seen any hard work since his father had sold the pigs and sent him to Maynooth. 'Not you, my son,' he added, looking at the Fairy Queen with anxious eyes.

The Fairy Queen smiled. His teeth were excellent and lit up his dark, handsome face like a lamp. 'Naturally not me, Father.' He looked at the Irish priest knowingly, his dark eyes full of the cynical sadness of his knowledge

The Priest extended his hand. 'This way please.'

There followed a seemingly endless

journey down long corridors, heavy with mahogany furniture and dark oil portraits of long-dead prelates. Finally he stopped in front of a huge intricately-carved door, from which pudgy cupids hung in naked abandon, blowing trumpets. Hesitantly he tapped. A soft voice said, 'Please enter.'

The priest grinned at them, as if he had achieved something. He opened the twin doors and indicated they should enter.

Facing the tall mullioned window, his back to them, a man in the long robe of a Monseigneur was standing.

'Here they are,' Father O'Leary said and waited hesitantly.

'Thank you, Father. You may go,' the cultivated English voice said.

The priest backed out and closed the door behind him. The Destroyers looked at each other in bewilderment and waited. For what seemed a long time the priest continued to stare out of the window – at what, they could not see.

Then Stevens's brow creased in a frown. He nudged Gippo. 'Hey nig-nog, do you see that?' he whispered.

'What?'

'The smoke. Look.' He indicated the thin blue smoke which was curling upwards.

'He's smoking a fag.'

'Of course he is, you old rogue Stevens. He couldn't do without his weeds, could he?'

The Monseigneur swung round, his robe swishing about his feet. Facing them, cigarette holder clenched between his teeth, Commander Miles Mallory allowed himself a faint detached smile at their open-mouthed surprise.

'Welcome to the Vatican City.'

'Oh, my aching back!' the Yank gasped.

SECTION THREE:
FIND BENITO MUSSOLINI

'If anyone can find Italy's man-of-destiny, it
will be Captain Skorzeny, believe you me.'
Commander Mallory of the Destroyers

CHAPTER ONE

'*Heil, mein Führer,*' the gigantic, scar-faced SS officer cried and raised his arm in rigid salute. '*Hauptsturmbannführer Skorzeny meldet sich zur Stelle!*'

Hitler looked up and, taking off his steel-rimmed spectacles that made him look like an elderly book-keeper, nodded. 'Good to see you again, Skorzeny.'

The head of the SS's special sabotage and spy commando remained at attention while the *Prominenz* of the Third Reich arranged themselves around the big table at Hitler's East Prussian HQ – the ex-champagne salesman, baggy-eyed Joachim von Ribbentrop, now foreign minister; Field-Marshal Keitel, as wooden, stupid and proud as ever; Admiral Dönitz, head of the German Navy; and Air Marshal Goering, laden down as usual with exotic decorations and medals. Himmler, the bespectacled former chicken farmer, nodded to Skorzeny. He could begin his report.

Skorzeny got off to a fumbling start. 'In

accordance with the orders of the Führer, I flew to Italy to discover the whereabouts of the Duce, now in the hands of Italian traitors,' he began, but Hitler interrupted him.

'We know that, Captain,' he said impatiently. 'Let us have your findings.'

'Yes, *mein Führer*.' Quickly he explained how he had traced the missing Duce to an island off the coast of Italy. 'Today he is located in the Villa Weber on the island, *mein Führer*, and we are confident that we can rescue him without difficultly – if we have your permission.'

Hitler considered a moment, then he nodded. 'Good, Skorzeny, if you think that you can get him off this island – what's its name again?'

'St Maddalena.'

'Off St Maddalena, without risking the Duce's life. You must realise, my old comrade must not be endangered in any way.'

'I understand, *mein Führer*,' Skorzeny said dutifully.

While the *Prominenz* gathered round, Skorzeny seized a pencil and sketched in the position of the island in relation to Italy and marked an X to designate the Villa in which the Duce, missing for over ten days now, was being held prisoner by his own police. 'As I see it, *meine Herren*,' he explained, 'with my own men and a company of SS volunteers from Corsica, I shall approach the island in a small flotilla of E-boats. At the same time we will send in a German naval squadron – on a courtesy visit.' He smiled and his illustrious listeners laughed; they could guess the purpose of that 'courtesy visit'.

'I see you are ahead of me, gentlemen,' Skorzeny said. 'And you are right. While the commander of the squadron is paying his respects to the local Italian naval commander, my E-boats will come in, covered by the guns of the squadron.' He pointed to the sketch map. 'We should be able to take the place before anyone realises what is happening. In essence, *meine Herren*, I'm relying on surprise and boldness to ensure success.'

He paused and noted with satisfaction that these men who controlled the destinies of ten million soldiers were nodding their approval at his plan.

For a moment Hitler stroked his little toothbrush moustache, that was as obviously dyed as his hair. Finally he said, 'I approve your plan, Skorzeny, and think it is practical – providing you act decisively.' He nodded to Dönitz. 'You take care of the necessary orders to the *Kriegsmarine*. Captain Skorzeny is to get the units he requires.'

Admiral Dönitz made a quick note. *'Jawohl, mein Führer.'*

Hitler turned to Skorzeny again. 'I have, however, to point out one thing to you, Captain Skorzeny. My friend Mussolini has to be rescued at once. Otherwise they will surrender him to the Allies. So I want the operation carried out soon. But understand that if you fail, I may have to disown you, since Italy is our ally – in name. I should have to say – for reasons of state – that you acted without orders. Your foolhardy action was prompted by excessive zeal, by ambition. If you fail, I must repudiate you. Skorzeny, you must accept this heavy responsibility for the sake of Germany!'

On the afternoon of 26 August, 1943, two sailors in the casual white uniform of the *Kriegsmarine* strolled aimlessly along the front of La Maddalena, past the local idlers who sprawled lazily in the shady waterfront bars, grateful for the slight breeze which came from the sea.

Skorzeny, the bigger of the two, was in a black mood. For twenty-nine days he had been hunting the Duce. Tomorrow the attack was scheduled to go into operation. And now he had discovered that his companion, Lieutenant Warger, had failed to mention that there was another telephone cable leading from the closely guarded Villa Weber. Fluently he cursed Warger as they moved towards their target for a last reconnaissance. Warger hung his head and said nothing. They strolled closer to their objective of the morrow. Skorzeny noted the double *carbinieri* guard which marched up and down the street and a further machine-gun post which had been built near the gate of the villa. Unfortunately the walls of the place itself were too high for him to see in. But the place did not look too tough a nut to crack. All the same he needed some insight into the ground floor layout of the house. That was the reason why they were here today. Warger had found a little house from which they could observe the villa from above.

Together they strolled into the dark interior of the whitewashed cottage. The middle-aged Italian woman in the typical ankle-length black woollen dress, wiped her reddened hands on her apron and muttered good day. Skorzeny nodded while Warger tipped his soiled duds on the laundress's scrubbed kitchen table, and muttered the usual phrases.

Then the big man began his act. He grimaced, groaned and grabbed his stomach. 'It's dysentery,' he groaned while Warger translated. 'Where's the latrine?'

The laundress launched into a voluble explanation, shrugging and pulling a shamefaced expression. She was a poor woman. Her house was poor too. There was no toilet.

As agreed upon beforehand Warger took his cue. 'There's a rockslide fifty metres up the road,' he told Skorzeny. 'I'll wait for you here.' Skorzeny mumbled something hurriedly to the woman and hurried off as if he had not a moment to spare or there would be a highly embarrassing incident.

Crouched behind a large rock, his white duck trousers lowered around his knees for the sake of realism in case some nosy *carbinieri* was observing him with his glasses, he peered down at the villa which housed Mussolini. The place was pompous and fake. Its walls of dark-coloured stone were adorned with terracotta lions and aggressive-looking eagles. But there was no sign of the Duce. Instead some twenty Italians strolled back and forth in the courtyard, some in their shirtsleeves, most of them without hats or weapons, completely unconcerned. Skorzeny grinned to himself, in spite of his uncomfortable position. Typically Italian. But all the same, as he remarked much later, 'everything seemed to be highly in order.'

Satisfied with the results of his little reconnaissance, he hitched up his trousers, still finding it difficult to do up the complicated button arrangement of the sailor pants, and strolled back to the laundress's house.

Warger and the woman were not alone any more. A *carbinieri* from the guard was standing in the kitchen chatting idly to the other two; he, too, had brought his laundry to be washed.

Skorzeny gave him a lazy good day and, offering the Italian a cigarette, started a conversation which Warger translated for him. He tried an old trick which Warger and he had used before to get information. Having won the policeman's confidence by lavishly praising everything Italian, he said sadly, 'But the Duce is unfortunately dead.

It is very sad.'

The policeman, who up to now had been passive and bored, shook his head violently. 'No,' he exclaimed, 'the Duce is not dead.'

'I know for a fact that he is,' Skorzeny said. 'I've had all details from a doctor friend of mine.'

'Yes,' Warger chipped in, 'the German radio in Berlin announced that he died of a fever this morning.'

The policeman laughed out loud. *'No, no, signore,'* he said energetically. *'Impossible!'* He waved his hands. 'I saw him myself this morning. I was part of his escort. We led him to the white seaplane.'

Skorzeny nodded. He had spotted the Red Cross rescue plane which had been anchored off the island for the last week as soon as they had arrived. 'Yes, yes,' he prompted.

'And I saw him being taken away in it,' the policeman ended his account.

Skorzeny turned round and looked out to sea. Indeed the plane had gone!

Then he realised that, although there were as many guards as ever at the Villa Weber, the stiffening had gone out of them. They were relaxed and careless. *Naturlich!* Their captive had flown the coop.

'Come on, Warger,' Skorzeny cried. 'We've got to get to a telephone!'

'Why?'

'To cancel the whole damn operation before they set off from Corsica!'

As the two pseudo-sailors raced down the hill towards the nearest café, where they hoped to find a telephone, a new question was rapidly assuming menacing proportions in Skorzeny's mind. Where the hell had they taken the Duce?

CHAPTER TWO

The Destroyers had been asking themselves the same question ever since Mallory had turned up in the Vatican and told them that their mission had been changed.

'Yes, it's me,' he said, amused by their surprised looks. 'I think it suits me rather well, don't you? Though it might be somewhat misunderstood in the swishier part of Shaftesbury Avenue. However, let me explain. It was the only thing the OSS people could dream up at short notice to get me into Rome. A Lysander could not have made it from Algiers to Rome and back and I certainly wasn't going to trust the 21st Transportation Wing to drop me by parachute after the ballsup they made of the Sicily drop. I'm afraid a lot of our chaps bought it on that one because they panicked and dropped them into the sea. But, to get back to myself, I arrived courtesy of the Special Boat Service. They landed me just off Reggio and I came the rest of the way dressed "thusly", as our American cousins would say. Monseigneur Kelly of the Vatican. Now let me tell you why I'm here. First, your mission has changed.'

'That's good, sir,' Crooke interrupted. 'Canaris knows all about phase two of Operation Mincemeat.'

'I know. The Fairy Queen told me. Thank God we arranged for the First Airborne to come in by sea! They'll be watching the probable air landing strips. But it really doesn't matter much anyway. Our people are already in Lisbon negotiating Italy's surrender with their generals. They'll be out of the war any day now. My guess is that our chaps will walk ashore at Taranto unopposed. It'll be one big picnic – unless the Boche take a hand in the business.'

'It looks like the beginning of the end,'

Crooke said.

The Commander shrugged. 'I don't know. The Boche still have plenty of tricks up their sleeves, as you'll soon hear. At all events it means the end of your mission. But you have a new one – one that might alter the whole course of the rest of the war in Europe.' He paused and allowed the silence to emphasise what he was about to say. 'Gentlemen, ever since early 1940 a top British Intelligence team has been able to read virtually every signal, every order, every message that has come out of Hitler's HQ by radio!'

The announcement had its effect. The Destroyers gasped.

'But how?' Crooke asked.

'Frankly, I don't quite know myself. The matter is ultra-secret. And although I know most things that go on in Intelligence, this is one that they've not informed me about. In fact, only a few people at the top of MI6 know – and they've all been vetted by C personally – and the respective heads of the three service intelligence set-ups, such as Admiral Godfrey. All I know is that in early 1939 one of our cipher people was asked to go to Warsaw by Polish Intelligence, in order to meet a young Polish mechanic who had been working in Germany in a hush-hush factory. The mechanic had a very interesting story to tell. At this hush-hush factory he'd had a row with the foreman and had been fired. A banal everyday story, you might say – save for one thing. He had been working on the enigma.'

'The what?'

'*Nomen es omen*. The enigma is the coding machine used in all top German head-quarters for coding their orders. And our Polish mechanic was no mug. Although for security reasons the Boche had allowed the workers on the production line to deal with one part only, he'd kept his eyes and ears open. He told our chap that he reckoned he could reconstruct the whole machine. Our man acted at once. The Pole was whisked out of the country and taken to Paris, where one of our MI6 men acted as his bodyguard while he rebuilt the enigma in wood. The final result was interesting enough to convince our people in London that they wanted the real thing. And with the Pole's help they got it just before the outbreak of war.'

He paused and lit another cigarette.

'What happened next, I don't know. In the DNI, only my chief knows. But what I *do* know is that we started to decode the first top-level Boche signals just before the Battle of Britain...'

'Well, I'll be buggered!' Stevens interrupted. 'Then we could have warned the civvies in London that the *Luftwaffe* was on its way?'

'Yes. That was a decision the PM had to take. The alternative was to tell the people and soon the Jerries would have found out from their agents in London and would have known we'd broken the code. Well, we've just discovered that Canaris knows that we've broken the enigma. Somehow or other he got on to the Polish Intelligence chap who first drew our attention to the mechanic. The Polish Underground let us know two weeks ago. But fortunately he has not revealed his knowledge to the High Command. Canaris is a very strange individual. C, who knows a lot about him through his contacts, says Canaris's mind is impenetrable. He has his fingers in so many pies that it's impossible to say on which side he is. For years he helped Hitler in his rise to power. But since 1939 he seems to have been up to his neck in the plot to get rid of him. The Gestapo know, yet for some reason they are biding their time. Why they don't arrest him, we simply do not know. But we do know that his nerve is beginning to break. Last year he approached C and suggested that the two heads of intelligence should meet in Lisbon. Imagine it, the two heads of enemy intelligence services meeting together in the middle of a total war! But Eden vetoed the idea, although C was quite prepared to go.'

'But what has this got to do with the enigma?' Crooke broke in.

'Well, this is the way we see it. So far Canaris has not reported his discovery to Hitler. Why? We see two possibilities. One, he's using it as some kind of insurance to save his skin, offering to forget the information if we bail him out by getting him out of Germany to some neutral country. But, I don't think that's the answer. And even if it is, we can't afford to wait till he makes the opening move. The other possibility is that Canaris is going to tell Hitler as soon as this Italian business is over. He knows well enough that Italy is going to get out of the war. After all his great friend, Amé, of the Italian Secret Service, is one of the conspirators! So, as soon as Hitler gets the news that the Eyeties are out of the war, Canaris will come along with his piece of information. Psychologically speaking, it will be a very opportune moment. Canaris will be reinstated and all this plotting against Hitler's life will be forgotten.'

'So you want us to get rid of Canaris?' Yank suggested.

'No,' Mallory shook his head. 'No, not at all! Canaris, we know, keeps a diary. It could well be that he has committed this information to it. If Canaris were killed it could well be that the diary would be in Hitler's hands, via the Gestapo, in a matter of hours and he'd know the whole business. No, our plan is different. We intend to compromise Admiral Canaris so completely that no one will ever believe anything he says again. We've got to push him so deep into the mire, that Hitler wouldn't believe him even if he came along bearing Winston Churchill's love life on a silver plate! Our people in Algiers concerned with the security of the enigma operation had no time for elaborately planned schemes. All they could think of was that somehow or other we should implicate Canaris in the plot to remove the Duce. After all Mussolini was Hitler's model and in spite of the failure of the Italian army, the Duce has remained Hitler's only real friend.'

'But how are you going to associate

Canaris with the Duce's downfall?' Crooke asked.

'Not *you* but *we*,' Mallory corrected. 'That's to be your job. The situation is this. This afternoon the Duce went to visit the King at his palace outside Rome. The Fairy Queen heard this evening that Mussolini never came back from that meeting. As far as we can find out, the King had already planned his arrest this morning. At all events, a special detachment of Italian police reported to the palace, ostensibly to keep a look-out for Allied paras, who might be dropped to kidnap the King. What apparently happened was that the King was not abducted but Mussolini was. The Fairy Queen's contacts report that the Duce was pushed into an Army ambulance just after tea and driven away at high speed, leaving his official car behind.'

'And then?'

'Then? Nothing. Mussolini has disappeared from the face of the earth.'

Crooke considered the information for a moment. 'Interesting, but how does this tie up with trying to compromise Admiral Canaris?'

'Can't you see? If we can find the place where the Eyeties are hiding the Duce, we can plant the evidence of Canaris's collusion there for the Germans to find when they finally rescue him.'

'But how do you know that Hitler *will* attempt to rescue Mussolini?'

Mallory grinned. 'We have our contacts in the German High Command, you know. And the word has already gone out. A certain *Haupsturmbannführer* Otto Skorzeny, a Viennese member of the *Leibstandarte,*★ has been given the task of finding Musso and rescuing him – at Hitler's express command.' He lit another cigarette. 'And if anyone can find Italy's man-of-destiny,' he emphasised the words ironically, 'it will be Captain Skorzeny, believe you me.'

CHAPTER THREE

July had given way to August. Working from the cover of the neutral Vatican city, the Destroyers sought the Duce's prison with the aid of the Fairy Queen's homosexual

★The premier SS division 'Hitler's Own Bodyguard' regiment.

agent network, which reached into the highest circles of both the Italian and German military. Helped by one of Carlo's contacts, whose lover was a high-ranking officer in General Student's* HQ, they were able to follow Skorzeny's progress around the coast of Italy as he searched for Mussolini.

On the day that Skorzeny realised that the Duce had been removed from La Maddalena and had cancelled the attack from Corsica, Mallory only just had time to stop a similar operation launched by the Special Boat Service and the OSS. 'As I see it,' he told them after a puzzled Father O'Leary had admitted them to the Monseigneur's office yet again, 'Skorzeny's going about it the wrong way. Someone high up in the Italian military hierarchy must be controlling the Musso business. Thus as soon as Skorzeny gets to know the place where the Eyeties are keeping the Duce the chap who's in charge moves him.' He pursed his lips thoughtfully and looked at the Destroyers, who had now been accepted

*General Student, the para-general who had driven the British from Crete in 1941, was in charge of the Mussolini operation.

in the Vatican community as part of the human flotsam of German and Italian deserters, as well as British POW escapees, now safely ensconced behind the Leonine Wall. 'Now what does that suggest to you?'

Stevens said, 'That Skorzeny's movements are being reported to the Eyeties, either from General Student's HQ or from that of the rozzer, who nicked us. What's his name?'

'*Obersturmbannführer* Kappler?'

'Ay, that's him.'

Mallory nodded his agreement. 'You're probably right, Stevens. But one thing is certain – the chap who is running this Mussolini op is right here in Rome. And we've got to find the sod – *soon!*'

Just over a mile away in his third floor office in the via Tasso, the German police attaché was slowly coming to the same conclusion, after he had sifted the mass of conflicting reports which had flooded his desk ever since he had first taken over the intelligence side of the search. By now he was able to make a fairly reliable assessment of the Duce's movements since his arrest. He had been sped to the Podgora Barracks. There he had spent the night. A *carbinieri* had given him that information. Then by chance he had bumped into a wholesale grocer who supplied customers on the coast near Gaeta. The grocer had heard from a German sergeant, who was courting an Italian housemaid, that a very high-ranking prisoner had been moved to the fortress island of Ponza, some thirty kilometres off the coast. Twenty-four hours later an astonished sergeant was facing his Führer in East Prussia explaining how he had seen the Duce shipped out of the port while the streets had been empty during an Allied air raid. Bit by bit, Kappler's blue folder labelled *'Geheime Reichssache'**, grew fat with details and reports. But still, just like his unknown opposite number Mallory, he did not know where the Duce was being kept prisoner, in spite of the aid being given him by Himmler's tame astrologers, hauled out of the concentration camps to discover Mussolini's whereabouts. And the Führer was breathing down his neck. A worried *Obersturmbannführer* Kappler knew that he would have to find the Italian leader soon – or face the consequences. And he knew only too well what they would be.

*Literally 'Secret Reich's Matter', i.e. 'top secret'.

Giggles finally gave him the lead he was looking for. Ever since the ex-Mafia man had betrayed the Destroyers to the Ovra, Kappler had realised how valuable Giggles was. In spite of the fact that the Ovra had gone to ground as soon as Mussolini fell, they were still an organization to be reckoned with; their sources of information remained unrivalled.

Thus it was that Kappler made a habit of driving out to the old Appian Way early each morning, ostensibly to indulge in his hobby of colour photography; in fact to meet Giggles, who refused to tell him where in Rome he was living.

On the morning of 1 September, he pulled his box-like military *Volkswagen* into the shade of a grove of olive trees and settled down to wait for Giggles, but in a very few minutes Giggles appeared, as if from nowhere. Kappler's sharp eyes told him at once that he had not walked far. The tips of his black shoes were free from dust; obviously he had parked his car somewhere close by and walked the last few yards.

They shook hands in the continental fashion.

'You are looking very smart,' Kappler said in English.

'Yeah, I've always been a kinda snappy dresser,' Giggles said, running his hands down his black pin-striped suit and straightening his broad white tie. 'Latest Eyetie stuff. Cost me a bundle.'

Kappler took a thick wad of worthless Italian lira from his pocket and held it in his hand. 'Have you anything for me, Giggles?'

Giggles shrugged carelessly, his eyes glued to the money. 'It depends,' he said.

'On what?'

'On what you're gonna do with that dough, Colonel.'

'But, my dear Giggles,' Kappler said, 'it's yours.'

Giggles reached out a greedy hand.

'But not yet. I'm sure you have something for me.'

Giggles thrust his hand in the pocket of his suit and pulled out a slip of paper. It was an official message form. He handed it to Kappler, who ran his eyes over it, translating as he did so: 'Security precautions round the Gran Sasso d'Italia have been completed.'

Giggles thrust his hand under Kappler's nose. 'The dough!' he said coldly. 'The mazuma.'

Kappler handed it over. 'One last thing,' he said, as Giggles turned to go. 'I wouldn't sell this information to anyone else, if I were you, Giggles.'

'Sure,' Giggles said easily. 'You can rely on me, Colonel.'

'*Ja*,' Kappler said to himself as Giggles walked away, 'I can rely on you. *Arschloch!*'

An hour later he was back in his office in the via Tasso with Skorzeny, studying a map of central Italy.

'That's it,' Skorzeny said. 'He must be up there!' And he traced in the area of the Monte Corno mountain in the Gran Sasso, the highest of the Apennines. 'It's an ideal place to keep anyone prisoner. Look at the contours. Three thousand metres above the plain.'

'But where exactly?' Kappler asked.

'At the Monte Corno, it's obvious. That hotel at the foot. That's where they're holding the Duce.'

Two kilometres away Giggles was already selling the information to one of General Amé's senior advisers. Again money changed hands. Then, when Giggles was safely gone, the senior adviser called a well-remembered number. 'Darling,' he drooled, 'I've got a wonderful piece of news for you – Carlo…'

CHAPTER FOUR

It was unbearably hot and the streets were deserted. The Romans had fled the city or had taken refuge behind shuttered windows and closed doors. Even the blind lottery ticket sellers and the pathetic ex-soldiers who usually displayed their stumps in the via Veneto had vanished. That afternoon it was abandoned to the dogs, who lay panting in the gutters, and to the Destroyers who sat and sweated inside the big black Fiat which Mallory had somehow 'borrowed' from the Vatican car pool.

Suddenly Gippo started. 'There is Giggles,' he whispered. And sure enough there he was, just leaving his new mistress's apartment. But it was a transformed Giggles. Now he wore a sober blue serge suit, a bowler hat and carried a pair of pearl-grey gloves. Unconcernedly, he strolled towards his car which he had parked in the shade further up the via an hour before.

'Now,' Crooke said. 'This is it!'

Thaelmann put his foot down and the car

shot forward. Hearing the noise Giggles turned in sudden alarm. He recognised the Destroyers at once, and hurled himself to one side. The car missed him by inches and he started to run back the way he had come, dodging in and out of the trees which lined the avenue.

Thaelmann swung the car round and charged forward again. The car lurched on to the pavement. *'Hold tight!'* he yelled.

Then they were roaring between the narrow line of trees. Giggles spun round, pulled his pistol from its shoulder holster and fired in one and the same movement. The windscreen shattered but the car hurtled on. Suddenly there was a bump followed by a scream. Thaelmann hit the brakes hard but he was too late. The bonnet of the car crumpled like a banana skin as it hit the tree.

Almost at once bedroom windows started opening and shutters were thrown back. Tousled sleepy heads began to appear. The Destroyers forced open the doors of the car. It was a total wreck and steam was pouring from the damaged radiator. But they had no eyes for the car; their gaze was fixed on the man lying at the foot of the tree behind them, blood seeping through his dark blue suit. Giggles was dying.

Stevens was first off the mark, then Yank, pistol in hand. A woman screamed when she saw the gun and disappeared swiftly from the open window. Crooke, running behind the first two, could guess where she was going – to telephone the *carbinieri*.

Yank grabbed Giggles and hit him hard across the face with his open hand. Across the road at a second-floor window, a man put his fingers in his mouth and whistled shrilly after the manner of an Italian football crowd. Yank hit Giggles again. 'Come on, you bastard! You're not croaking till you tell us where they're hiding Mussolini!' Viciously he shook the dying man. 'I said – speak,' he yelled.

Giggles spoke, but his voice was barely audible. 'Gran Sasso ... Hotel Imperatore ... sacrament,' he whispered, 'a priest ... I can't go without.'

'Rot in hell, you bastard!' the Yank snarled as a police car squealed round the corner. Angry Italian voices shouted directions and whistles blew as the Destroyers scattered and ran.

In the gutter Giggles lay still.

Commander Mallory hitched up the skirt of

his robe and said, 'Bloody nuisance.' Then he turned to the big map of the Apennines and central Italy. 'All right, then if you'll pay attention.' The Destroyers put down their glasses and turned towards him. 'So it looks pretty genuine. The Campo Imperatore Hotel is located here at the foot of Monte Corno, the highest peak in the Apennines, covered in snow all year round.' He tapped the map again, while the Destroyers sipped their ice-cold beer. 'The hotel is a modern place, according to my information. A favourite place with Italian skiers, although it has one great disadvantage – at least for skiers. Sole access to the place is by funicular railway which runs up 3,000 feet from the village of Assergi – here.'

'But it makes an ideal place for hiding the Duce,' the Fairy Queen said. 'Only one way in. Easy to guard.'

'You're quite right, Carlo,' Mallory answered. Most unexpectedly he rather liked the handsome queer. 'An ideal place too for defensive action. That's why the Italians picked it for his hiding place.'

'But what now, sir?' Crooke asked. 'Do we know that the Germans will try to rescue Mussolini? Secondly, if they do, how will they do it? And, finally, how are we going to get up there if the only way up is by the funicular railway?'

Commander Mallory smiled. For the first time in many days he felt relaxed, now that they knew the Duce's whereabouts. He turned to the Fairy Queen. 'Okay, Carlo, what do you know?'

'General Student is at Pratica di Mare airfield just outside Rome. He is accompanied by a young paratroop Major called Mars or Mors. I do not know exactly.' He turned to Crooke. 'You get the picture?'

'Yes, a para-drop on the hotel itself. A tricky business, I'd say. A para-drop at that height without ground support! The danger from aircurrents alone up there is pretty extreme. I wouldn't like to tackle it. Do you really think the Jerries would attack it from the air?'

'What else can they do?' said Mallory. 'Hitler is obviously breathing down Skorzeny's neck and he's prepared to take risks. And most of Skorzeny's SS commandos are para-trained. And what do we make of the major's presence – Mars or Mors or whatever his name is?'

'Okay, I'll buy the para-drop, though it seems awfully risky to me. But how the devil are we to get to the Duce and plant the evidence before Skorzeny and his bully boys make their landing if the only way up is by the funicular railway?'

Mallory crooked a finger at him. 'Have a look at this.'

Crooke craned forward to stare at the large scale map of the mountain range, while the Destroyers crowded in behind him to peer over his shoulder.

Mallory tapped the map. 'The Eyeties, as we know from Carlo here, have thrown a strong cordon of troops around the base of the mountain. Perhaps two battalions in all. At all events all the roads leading up the Assergi Valley station where the funicular is, are sealed off, though I don't doubt you and your chaps will be able to get through the cordon without too much trouble and make your way up to Assergi. But then your headaches really start. Even if you managed to get aboard the cable car, the Eyeties could cut off the power and leave you stranded halfway up the mountain.'

Gippo gulped audibly at the thought and the others grinned; they knew his dislike of heights well enough by now.

'So there is another way?' Crooke prompted.

Mallory nodded. 'Right, there's a

mountain trail which runs up to the hotel. You can see it on this old map. It was used by the builders of the hotel and was abandoned once the funicular had been built.'

'And how do we know that the trail can still be used?'

'You don't,' the Commander answered. 'You don't! But it's the only hope you've got of getting up that bloody mountain.'

'All right. How much time do we have to carry out the op before Skorzeny's paras drop?'

Mallory turned to Carlo. 'What do you say?'

The Italian shrugged eloquently. 'My friend, he says that the Germans are waiting for aeroplanes from Southern France. I do not know exactly. Two, perhaps three days at the most.'

CHAPTER FIVE

Kappler was the first to make his report, while Student, plump, red-faced and jovial, and Skorzeny, gigantic and grim, stood at the side of the big conference room, filled with the officers of the Airborne Corps, and listened intently. 'We are now sure that it is the Campo Imperatore, gentlemen,' he said precisely. 'Things are definitely moving up there. My agents tell me that the *carbinieri* have set up check points on all roads and all the local staff of the hotel have been fired without notice.' He smiled. 'Hence they were only too prepared to air their grievances to my people. I have also quizzed General Soleti of the Rome *carbinieri*. Indeed I called him a liar for denying he knew where the Duce is. They forced the information out of him that on the day before yesterday the Duce was still imprisoned there. So we can conclude that – unless the Italians get wind of our operation – he's still in the hotel.' He sat down amid a murmur of interest.

Skorzeny strode over to the map. 'Let me tell you first that the information on which we are basing this operation, gentlemen, is not very accurate or up to date. The Führer has vetoed any action which would tip the scales in Italy against the Third Reich. Hence we could only make two hasty overflights in the Gran Sasso area. These are the results.' He pulled a string and the curtain next to the big relief map slid back to reveal a series of smudgy eight by eight-inch prints. 'Perhaps you could all come a little closer.'

There was a scraping of chairs and a shuffle of feet as the assembled officers moved forward and craned their necks to examine the poor prints, which had been obviously photographed under difficult circumstances.

One of the *Luftwaffe* pilots whistled softly. 'Doesn't look so good, *Hauptsturm*,' he said. 'Is that the hotel?' he pointed to a dark smudge in the left-hand corner of one of the prints.

Skorzeny nodded, but said nothing. The pilots did not realise what a risk he had taken to get that photograph – hanging out of a Heinkel at 4,000 feet, his hands numb in the icy air while a crew member had hung on to his waist. The officers stared at the lunar landscape around the hotel.

'Where's the landing zone in that mess?' one of them asked.

'There,' Skorzeny explained, pointing to the only flat patch. 'That's the spot we've chosen.'

Then General Student spoke. '*Meine Herren*, I do not need to tell you that we must risk this operation on the basis of defective data. But it is vital we carry it out. The Führer desires it. Now this is the plan. At midday on Sunday, 12 September, your Heinkels will take off towing a dozen DFS 230 gliders. Each glider will contain the pilot and ten other men, drawn from Major Mors's battalion.' He indicated a square-faced soldier in the corner, who was dressed in the baggy coveralls of a paratrooper. 'Or from Captain Skorzeny's special commando. All in all we will have one hundred and eight combat soldiers at our disposal for the mission. One hour later the force should be over the Gran Sasso. The tugs will then release their gliders at about one thousand metres. It will be the task of their occupants to seize the hotel and rescue the Duce. While this operation is going on, the remainder of the para battalion under Major Mors will capture the Assergi station of the funicular.'

'But, sir,' one of the pilots said, 'do you think the gliders will have any chance whatsoever? What happens if the DFSs meet thermals? They could turn a DFS over just like that!' He snapped his finger and thumb.

Student had been told that very morning by his experts that he could expect eighty per cent casualties among his glider crews, but he kept that pessimistic information to himself. 'You don't need to lecture me on the subject, Captain. I was flying gliders back in 1920 when you were still piddling in your trousers.'

The remark caused a welcome burst of laughter. The captain's face flushed a deep red.

'This operation will be a success. As long as you all keep your nerve – it'll be like a peacetime manoeuvre. As I see it, the surprise will be so great that probably not a shot will be fired at you by the Italians. Your problem will be solely to concentrate on your landing sites, and keeping to them to avoid crashing into each other.'

Student caught the sidelong looks the pilots gave each other. He knew what was going through their heads. He had crashed his own first glider back in 1920: he knew how they all felt. But he knew too, that gliders were the only answer. Air currents would swirl paratroopers to their deaths on the rocks below Monte Corno. Gliders were the lesser risk.

'Once we've landed,' Skorzeny took up the narrative, 'we'll go in without any firing. Indeed our soldiers will be given strict orders *not* to fire, because of the danger to the Duce's life, unless I fire a Very light to indicate Italian resistance. If they do decide to fight then we shall pin them down with machine guns and mortars until we can convince them to surrender. Now any further questions?'

The young captain who had asked about the gliders' chances of success plucked up courage again. 'All right, let us assume that you can land successfully, free the Duce as planned, and so forth, what do you do about getting him off the mountain, if all the roads below are covered by the Macaronis?'

Skorzeny looked at Student enquiringly but the latter shook his head.

'I'm afraid I'm not at liberty to divulge that piece of information, Captain, even to you. Let us say that like the fellow in the Greek legend, he might grow wings and fly away.'

SECTION FOUR:
THE RESCUE

'Duce, the Führer has sent me! You are free!' *Otto Skorzeny to Benito Mussolini 12 September, 1943*

CHAPTER ONE

'Okay, Thaelmann, let's stop here,' Crooke ordered, his mouth full of dust. 'There's some cover over there.'

As the rutted third-class road breasted the long incline, Thaelmann pulled the stolen *Abwehr* car over to the verge. He switched the engine off and the ancient Horch, which Carlo had stolen from his master, shuddered, a cloud of steam coming from its overheated radiator.

The Destroyers got out, stamping their feet on the road. 'Thank God for that,' Stevens said wearily. 'I thought we was never going to stop.'

'Gippo,' Crooke ordered, 'fill the radiator up again.'

'Not much use bothering, sir,' Thaelmann said, looking up from a stale salami sandwich. 'The engine's dry. We've no more juice.'

Crooke accepted the news calmly. The stolen car had about served its purpose. They were almost there now.

'Is that it, sir?' Peters asked.

'Yes, that peak over there – the one with the snow still on it – that's Monte Corno.'

They stared across the valley at the mountain. Its side rose almost vertically so that it seemed to be spread out before them like a map with paths, tracks, roads stretched over it like marker tapes. There appeared to be no movement on its slope, but Crooke knew that was deceptive. Everywhere up there were Italian soldiers – the best the country still had left – prepared to die to keep the man they had learned to hate so vehemently behind bars.

'It looks a big bugger,' Yank said.

'It is,' Crooke agreed. 'But let's get the car covered up and then into the shade to discuss our next move.'

In a matter of minutes they had camouflaged the car with olive branches and crawled into the shade of the olive grove. They squatted on the hot stones from which emerald lizards streaked in rapid zig-zags.

Stevens breathed out heavily and mopped his brow. 'It's warmer than up the ruddy blue!'

'I think it is nice, this warmth,' Gippo said with a bright smile.

'You bloody nig-nogs never notice it!'

Stevens said. 'You haven't been down from the trees long enough.'

Crooke smiled wearily. 'All right, pay attention. According to my map, we're about twenty kilometres from Assergi, where the funicular is. With a bit of luck we should be able to manage it during the dark. As I see it, we've got to be beyond the village before dawn – again with a bit of luck, and we'll need luck all right. All that Commander Mallory could supply me with by way of a map indicates the main roads only. Naturally, they'll be guarded. As for the secondary roads and tracks.' He shrugged. 'That's anybody's guess.'

'So we play it by ear, eh?' Yank said.

'Well, whatever that means, yes I suppose we do.' He turned to Peters. 'You take the first hour's stag. I'll relieve you at four. The rest of you get your heads down. It's going to be a long night.'

Slowly but inevitably the big car, its engine drained completely dry, came to a stop, as Thaelmann steered it into a grove of olives at the side of the track. 'The end of the road, gentlemen,' he said and put on the brake. Their downhill coasting was over.

'All out,' Crooke ordered, 'and keep quiet.

As far as I know this road is patrolled. At least we've got to assume it is.'

It was completely dark now. The valley at the base of the mountain was silent save for the ever-present noise of the cicadas. In single file, spread out with three feet between each man, they moved off briskly. The thick dust muffled the sound of their boots; it would also muffle the approach of any patrol.

They had been marching for over an hour when they struck the first Italian outpost – a stone shepherd's hut at the side of the track. Carefully they worked their way round it, the chatter of the guards within clearly audible. When they had cleared it, Crooke pulled his pistol and checked the catch. 'Gippo,' he whispered, 'pass the word back. Everyone to have his gun ready, but not to use it unless absolutely forced.'

The hours went by slowly. They marched at a steady four miles an hour, each one of the Destroyers wrapped in his own thoughts, concentrating on the track, which was growing increasingly steeper. The temperature started to drop, which was a relief, and a half moon, sliding from behind the clouds, illuminated their way.

Just before midnight, as they were working

their way round a patch of cactus, they heard the crunch of steel-shod boots on the trail above them. Forty, fifty feet away at the most. Like grey wolves, the Destroyers sank into the shadows on both sides of the track. Just in time. A steel-helmeted young soldier swung round the bend, automatic rifle slung over his shoulder. Behind him came another – and another.

Crooke lined his pistol up on the first man. Next to him he heard the click of Gippo's knife spring. Suddenly Crooke's heart missed a beat. 'Dogs,' he whispered.

Behind the third policeman, the handler fought to keep control of the leash holding back the two great dogs.

'Oh, my God!' Crooke said to himself, as he recognised them. They weren't just ordinary German shepherds, they were Dobermann Pinschers.

Suddenly the closer of the two hounds sniffed the air, its muzzle slightly open to reveal its big yellow teeth. Its handler said something in Italian and tugged at the leash with all his strength. The dog did not seem to notice. Instead it lowered its head and bared its teeth as it turned towards where they were hiding.

The first soldier stopped. 'What's going

on?' he enquired. 'Why are you stopping?'

'I don't know, Sergeant,' the handler said. 'The bitch won't move.' He pulled at the leash again with all his strength. 'What the devil's the matter with you?'

Suddenly it broke loose and hurtled forward, rising in a shallow dive for the two men hidden behind the cactus. But Gippo was quicker. In that same instant, he threw his knife. With a howl the big dog dropped, the knife sunk up to the hilt in its breast.

'Get 'em!' Crooke yelled. 'No firing!'

The Destroyers broke cover. Immediately the Italian soldiers grabbed for their weapons, frantic fingers searching for the safety catches. In an instant all was confusion, with the Destroyers and the Italians swaying back and forth in desperate man-to-man combat.

'No noise,' Crooke hissed, 'We–'

The words died on his lips as the other dog launched itself at him. One hundred pounds of muscle and flesh hit him hard and bowled him over. He felt the dog claw his face, drawing blood, and he threw up his hands to protect his throat. Just in time he caught the animal's lower jaw as it thrust at his neck. Its teeth clamped down on his hand. He screamed with pain, but he didn't let go. Desperately, the animal struggled to free itself, raking Crooke's stomach with its back legs, ripping his shirt to pieces. Crooke hung on as the Dobermann Pinscher threw itself from side to side. Exerting all his strength he grabbed the animals' upper jaw, forced it closed, clamping his hands over its nostrils at the same time. The dog squirmed back and forth but Crooke held fast while all around him the grim battle went on. Suddenly the dog threw itself on one side. The move took Crooke completely un- awares and his hands slipped from its jaws. The Dobermann gave a vicious grunt, squirmed to its feet and launched itself at Crooke's throat. But it never got there. Peters dived forward, an Italian bayonet gleaming in his upraised hand. He landed on the animal's back – all thirteen stone of him. The dog collapsed under the Guards- man's weight and before it could squirm free, the Guardsman drove his bayonet into its back. A stream of blood shot up, drench- ing the Guardsman's shirt. He thrust the bayonet home once more and the animal went limp.

Crooke rose groggily. His hands hurt like hell but he had no time for them. He cocked his head to one side, but there was no sound to be heard. The night had closed over the brief struggle to the death as swiftly as water over a stone. Wearily he said, 'Push the bodies in the ditch.' Swaying slightly, he watched as they did so, Yank not deigning even to touch the men he had killed. Instead he used his boot to roll them off the track to the steep slope of the drainage ditch. As usual he seemed completely unmoved by the scene of mayhem and murder. 'All right then,' Crooke ordered, when they were finished. 'Come on, let's be getting on. We've got a long way to go yet.'

CHAPTER TWO

Three hours later Thaelmann spotted the Germans. They were crouched on a rocky outcrop overlooking the little cluster of white-painted houses which made up the village of Assergi when Thaelmann said, 'Listen, that's German down there!'

The Destroyers strained their ears to pick up the sound. A moment later they saw the first German as he came out of the trees, crouched low, a sub-machine gun tucked into his hip. The stunted olives, bent by the prevailing wind, were full of similar shapes. 'German paras,' Peters whispered to Crooke. 'Tell 'em from their helmets.'

Crooke glanced at the luminous dial of his watch. It was nearly four. In an hour it would be dawn and then the Jerries would attack.

'What are they up to, sir?' Stevens asked. 'I thought Carlo said they was going to drop on old Musso's prison.'

'They are. But these lads are here to capture the base station of the funicular. When Skorzeny has freed Musso they're obviously going to bring him down by the cable car. Those fellows in the trees must have sneaked through the Italian patrols like we did.'

'And what now?' Yank said.

'We've got to change our plan. We haven't time to find the trail Mallory told us about. It would take too long. We've got to get our skates on and get to the hotel as quickly as possible. And there's only one way to do it.'

'The funicular?' Stevens asked.

'Yes.' Swiftly Crooke explained his improvised plan. 'Jerry'll probably attack at dawn. He always does on jobs like this. The sentries will be caught off guard thinking the night's duty is over and the rest will be fast asleep in their beds. So when the Jerries go in, we go in too, heading for the funicular, and we've got to get there before they do.'

'And then what?' Yank asked.

Crooke licked his dry cracked lips. 'Then? Well, then, we'll play it by ear.'

At 5.10 precisely there was a hiss, a soft crack and a blinding light burst over the red-roofed houses. Almost on the instant, a heavy machine gun chattered into life followed a second later by the burr of a machine pistol.

'They're going in!' Crooke yelled. 'Come on!'

They jumped to their feet. Before them the line of German paras were rushing the village, from which came frantic cries of surprise and alarm. Another machine gun opened up. This time it was Italian. The Destroyers could tell it from the German by its slower rate of fire. A para in front of them groaned, flung up his arms and pitched face forward into a stream. Close by another Italian machine gun started to fire at the paras. Another German fell screaming. Suddenly the paras were dropping all around them. Whether they were hit or just taking cover, Crooke did not know. All he knew was that the Italian machine-gunner, firing from what looked like a barn, had them pinned down.

Crooke cursed as he dropped to the ground. He buried his head into the dust as another burst swept the area. In a few minutes it would be fully light and then the Germans would discover them in their midst. 'Yank – Thaelmann!' he yelled desperately, 'get that bloody gun out of the way!'

'Us?' Yank said.

'Yes, *you!* Get on with it!'

'But we'll be helping the Krauts!'

'I don't bloody care. If we don't get it out of the way in a minute, we're gonners. Here.' He pulled out two of the precious Italian egg grenades, which Carlo had stolen for them from the Vatican's Swiss Guard arsenal. Yank grabbed the grenades.

Ten yards apart, the two Destroyers crept forward from the flank, dropping and remaining motionless while the Italian sprayed the area with lead, then dashing forward again once the tracer had gone. Suddenly the machine-gunner stopped firing. Still the paras hugged the ground. Perhaps the man who had been killed first had been their section leader. For the moment anyway they seemed leaderless and incapable of offensive action.

As the Destroyers wormed their way closer and closer to the barn, Crooke felt himself biting his bottom lip. Why the hell didn't the Eyetie open up again so that Yank could spot his firing slit? It was still too dark to locate it without the aid of his muzzle flash.

Twenty yards away from the squat straw-roofed outline of the barn, Yank was thinking the same thing. But he was equal to the situation. 'Okay, Kraut,' he whispered, as they crouched in the dirt, 'take this.' He handed him a handful of gravel. 'Move over there. When I shout "now", pitch it at the wall. You read me?'

'Yes, I read you.' Thaelmann stuck his pistol in his belt and crawled to the left.

Yank followed his progress tensely. Thaelmann stopped and turned. He knew exactly how dangerous his task was. He would have to raise his upper body to throw the gravel. If he didn't duck quickly enough, the Italian machine gunner could saw him in half at that range.

'NOW!' the Yank yelled.

He flung the gravel hard. It clattered against the side of the barn like small-arms fire and the Italian reacted immediately. A

182

spurt of tracer cut the air as Thaelmann ducked. The burst ended, but Yank had spotted the slit. He rose and lobbed with the easy bored grace of a professional ball player. The grenade sailed through the air, directly through the narrow slit.

For what seemed an age, nothing happened. Then there was a muffled explosion, followed by a frenzied scream. A cloud of smoke flooded through the slit. A moment later the barn door was flung open and a blackened figure staggered out and collapsed screaming in the dust.

The paras rose as one man and surged forward into the village, firing from the hip. The Destroyers needed no invitation. They ran after them, swinging towards the yellow light of the funicular station.

'Bloody hell,' Yank cursed, 'that's the first goddamn time I've fought for the Krauts!'

'Perhaps Hitler'll give yer the iron cross! Come on!' Stevens gasped.

Now the firing was becoming more sporadic. They sprang over a dead Italian sprawled out in the middle of the road. And another. In between the houses the paras were shouting to one another in excited triumph. They realised they were winning. Just before the funicular station, Crooke collided with a young German para, his excited face streaked with sweat. '*Da seid ihr–*' the words of welcome died on his lips when he saw that these were not his comrades. He opened his mouth to shout for help but he never managed it. Gippo stuck his knife into the man's throat and ripped it upwards remorselessly. His face contorted with terror and agony; the German went down, the blood welling up and choking him. Gippo pulled out his knife and wiped it on the dying man's coveralls before running on after the others. Then they were inside the station. An elderly white-faced *carbinieri* sergeant stood there, pistol held in his shaking hand. Crooke chopped down his clubbed fist. The pistol clattered to the metal floor. 'How does it work?' he rapped in poor Italian. 'Function?' The sergeant was so terrified that he could not speak. He opened his lips to form the words, but no sound came. Crooke hit him on the chin and he went down, unconscious before he hit the floor. 'The telephone,' he ordered and Thaelmann pulled the old-fashioned crank phone off the wall. From close by came the clatter of hob-nailed boots.

'The paras are coming up the path!'

Stevens yelled. 'Quick – inside!'

They clambered in the big cage and Crooke pressed the blue start button while Peters crashed home the door. But nothing happened.

Horrified cries came from outside as the paras discovered their murdered comrade.

'The outer gate!' Stevens yelled. 'We've got to close the outer gate!'

Crooke jerked back the door again as a bullet whined past the door post, missing Crooke by inches. He grabbed the outer grid, slammed it home and flung the inner door closed. Stevens pressed the blue button again; there was a whirring of machinery and with a rusty squeak and a jerk the cage began to ascend. The wall of the shed slid past and disappeared.

They jumped back from the centre of the cage as bullets stitched an angry line right across the wooden floor. A gust of icy air burst in as Yank smashed one of the windows with his pistol butt. Reaching out he dropped the other Italian grenade on the men below.

'Achtung!' someone yelled and the paras scattered. There was a crash as one wall of the shed blew out and then the firing stopped. They were on their way.

CHAPTER THREE

The funicular car rocked and swayed alarmingly whenever the wind caught it. Above them the ill-maintained wheels screeched and grated in shrill cacophony. The wind whistled through the splintered bullet holes in the floor and the wooden body work creaked and protested like a ship ploughing through a heavy sea.

Crooke peered through the shattered window at the view. The sun was sliding out from behind the jagged peaks, throwing a shadow across the mountainside. He strained his neck in an attempt to make out just where the hotel lay, but he could not see it.

'What are you looking for, sir?' Stevens asked.

'The hotel!'

'Do you think they'll be waiting for us then, sir?'

'I should think they'll have a permanent guard on the station up there. And we haven't got this far to be pipped at the post.

Somehow or other we've got to get out of this damned thing without being seen.' He craned his head to look down at the valley.

Gippo followed his example and gripped the rail frantically when he saw the drop. 'I am being sick when I see it,' he said.

Crooke grinned sympathetically and swayed across to the door. Exerting all his strength, he pulled. It opened a few inches, then stopped. He let go and stepped back, gasping for breath. 'That's no good. There must be some kind of safety device which prevents the door being opened during the trip. And even if we could get it open, the Italians would spot we had done so and come looking for us. We don't want that. No one is to know we're up there.' He touched the precious documents which had been sewn into the lining of his jacket. 'It would be obvious that we had had a hand in framing Canaris.'

'What about the windows?' Thaelmann asked.

'No deal. They're too narrow. And the Eyeties might see us dropping out. After all we can only drop out when we're above ground and that's roughly when we get close to the station.' He fell silent and pondered the problem, staring at the bullet-holed floor from which the fresh splinters stuck up raggedly. 'Of course!' he said suddenly. 'That's it – the floor!'

'What do you mean, sir?' several voices asked at once.

'That's the way out,' he said. 'Through the floor. If we are below this thing as it comes up to the station, we might be able to drop without being seen.'

Hastily they set to work, digging their knives into the soft wood, tugging and pulling. With a grunt, Peters and Yank pulled up the first plank. Down below the valley came suddenly into view. But they had no time for it. The car was beginning to lose speed.

A second plank followed and a third. Crooke left them to it and crossed to the smashed window. The view was blotted out by the side of the mountain. 'Hurry it up!' he yelled over his shoulder. 'We're nearly there now.'

Finally they had a large enough gap for one man at a time to pass through. Crooke looked down at it and bit his lip. Someone would have to go out now if they were all to escape without being seen. He steeled himself. 'All right,' he said, 'I'm going first. Stevens, you follow me. Gippo, you'll be glad to know you're last.'

Crooke sat down and put out his right foot into space. He felt the wind grip it. He gritted his teeth and lowered the other one. With his right foot, he groped beneath the car until he found a hold on one of the metal supports. He put all his weight on it. It held. 'I'm off,' he said and looked up, catching a last glimpse of their anxious faces, as he lowered himself through the gap.

The next moment he was through and the wind was lashing at his face, sucking the breath from his lungs. He looked down and saw that he was about two hundred feet above the ground. He squirmed his body parallel to the base of the car and got a precarious hold on the girder with his other foot. He let go of his hold with his right hand and sought for a hold on the dirty greasy underneath of the car. He found something, cold, rough and metallic and gripped it. Then he hauled himself across to the girder on which he had rested his feet. The cable car had slowed down considerably now and was about fifty feet above the ground. He braced himself for the drop. To his right, Stevens squirmed through the gap. He was smaller and much more agile than

Crooke and found a hold on the opposite girder quickly and clung there. Thaelmann followed.

They were about twelve feet above the rocks now. Crooke braced himself. 'Go!' he yelled, the wind tearing the word out of his mouth, and dropped. He hit the rough ground hard, the shin of his right leg striking against a boulder. Stevens followed the next instant. He gave a stifled yell of pain as he hit the ground a few feet away. Thaelmann came after him. One by one, as if they were dropping from the practise dummy at Ringway, the Destroyers left the car, leaving it to arrive at its destination empty.

The Hotel Campo Imperatore was silent, save for the clatter of pans in its basement as the cooks began to prepare breakfast. On the big terrace of the big white horseshoe-shaped building a blue-uniformed *carbinieri* guard was slumped over the back of a wooden chair, his rifle leaned against the wall next to him, his head bent in sleep.

Crooke turned to them. 'Now we've got to find the chappie in charge of the guard – Musso's senior warder, if you like – and plant the evidence against Canaris on him so that when the Germans get in, they're sure to find it.' He reached into his jacket and ripped at the lining. It came away easily to reveal the thin wedge of papers, wrapped carefully in an oilskin pouch.

'What are they exactly?' Gippo asked.

'Well, as far as Commander Mallory told me, a copy of the discussion which took place in Lisbon last year between the MI6 representative there and Admiral Canaris, plus his own note thanking the man for his time and trouble. A very indiscreet note on Canaris's part, I would say. A letter from General Eisenhower to General Amé, thanking the latter for his help in arranging peace negotiations between the Italians and the Allies, plus a letter from Amé on his official stationery, stolen by Carlo by the way, stating that he had the full support of Admiral Canaris in all his efforts, including his attempts to get rid of the Duce, which three documents should signify the end of Admiral Canaris's career with the German secret service.' He tapped them thoughtfully, not aware that one vital document within the yellow oilskin package was unknown to him – yet. 'The problem now is to find the chief guard and plant them on him.'

'Yeah, we can't just walk into the darned place and ask for the top guy,' the Yank agreed somewhat grumpily. The drop had re-opened the wound in his head where Giggles had hit him and it was bleeding again.

Stevens sniffed superciliously. 'We don't need to know, do we, Gippo?'

Gippo's dark eyes sparkled. 'No, I have experiences of such things. In the olden days I am always asking myself where the best people are staying in the hotels–'

'Yer, where do the big nobs hang out?' Stevens interrupted. He held up his dirty scratched hands in warning. 'And I don't want any dirty answers from you evil-minded lot, cos I'll blush. Where? The poshest room – that's where. That's in peacetime, of course. In wartime, the officers and gents, they do the same. The more rank they have, the bigger the room. Stands to reason, don't it?'

They nodded.

'So where's we going to find his nibs?'

Gippo answered the question for him. 'That place there with the big window on the two floor,' he said in his strange English. 'And above it to the rightish, that one on the three floor.'

Stevens smiled with approval. 'Smart lad –

for a wog!' He turned to Crooke. 'Me and Gippo'll go and have a look-see, sir. When we find him, we'll plant the evidence.'

'But why just you two?'

'Well, if you'll excuse me saying so, sir, we're the professionals. I mean that bunch of layabouts,' he indicated the other Destroyers, 'are all right for kicking in some sodding Jerry's back-teeth and that sort of rough stuff. But when it comes to the fancy work–' He broke off and did not finish his sentence. Instead he braced his finger-nails and breathed on them, as if he were about to polish them.

'Up yours!' Yank growled.

Crooke grinned. He realised Stevens was right. 'Okay, we'll try to cover you the best we can. But make it as quick as possible. Things are starting to move in there. We haven't got much time.'

'Leave it to us, sir.'

'And if you have any trouble, shout.'

'Don't worry, sir, we will.' And with that the two of them slipped away and were soon hurrying across the lawn.

Stevens nudged Gippo. His lips formed the word 'now'. While Stevens watched the silent dark corridor, Gippo inserted a piece of stiff plastic between the lock and the door jamb. He gave a grunt as he exerted pressure. The lock clicked suddenly and the door opened. Gippo slipped away the plastic and drew his knife. Cautiously he opened the door more widely. It creaked, but the sound of gentle snoring coming from within continued. The occupant of Room 101 on the second floor had not been wakened by the slight noise.

They crept in. A bald-headed old man slept in the big double bed, his back turned towards them. Stevens made signs to Gippo to indicate that he should check the room. They split up and searched it noiselessly for information as to the rank of its owner. Hastily they went through the small hallway with its hatstand and wardrobe, which contained nothing but a shabby blue suit. Stevens glanced into the tiled bathroom. Nothing there either. He turned his attention to the bedroom again. On the table there was a silver-framed photograph of a plumpish young man in pilot's uniform, but nothing which indicated the man gently snoring on the bed was anyone important.

Suddenly he froze. The sleeper's snoring ended in a stifled grunt. The big bed creaked under his weight. Stevens felt his jaw tighten. His hand holding the American pistol was suddenly hot with sweat. Then he relaxed; the man had not opened his eyes. He began to snore again.

Suddenly he realised who the sleeping man was. He had seen that sallow face with its great unshaven chin and glistening dome of a head often enough in newsreels.

'Gippo,' he whispered. 'You know who that is, don't yer? *It's old Musso himself!*' Hastily he grabbed the half-breed's arm. 'Come on, let's get out of here. We're looking for his keeper.'

In their haste Gippo almost fell over the little case, bearing the initials 'BM', which stood in the hall. Moments later they were out into the corridor again, hurrying up to the third floor. This time the big room on the third floor turned out to be the right one. A skinny sallow man was stretched out naked on the bed, his coverlet thrown back as the sun's first rays began to penetrate the half-drawn blind. But their eyes were not for him; they were for the blue uniform thrown casually over the big chair near the bed.

On tip-toe Stevens crossed the room to it. Swiftly he picked up the jacket, glanced at the mass of gold braid, then ran his fingers expertly through the pockets. He pulled out a pass. Flicking it open, he read the name

'Giuseppe Gueli' and then the rank below the name 'Inspector General of the *Carbinieri*'. He dropped it back into the pocket. Raising his thumb to the waiting Gippo to indicate that this was their man, his lips formed the word 'case'.

Gippo crossed to the big scratched wardrobe and opened it. It squeaked slightly. Stevens spun round. The naked man on the bed stirred, but he did not open his eyes. He nodded to Gippo. The half-breed pulled out a big black leather case. Stevens shook his head. Gippo bent again and took out a smaller one. Again his companion shook his head. 'Too big,' his lips formed the words, although no sound came. Then Gippo dug out a small slim briefcase. Stevens nodded. 'Yes, that's it,' he mouthed the words.

Suddenly he had an idea. Pulling the Inspector General's pass out of his pocket, he grabbed Gippo's arm and hurried him out of the room. With the door closed behind him, his eyes flickering up and down the empty corridor guardedly, he whispered, 'I've just had a great idea. If they get Musso out – the Jerries, I mean – they're only going to let him have his main gear – shaving stuff, important papers and so on, right?'

'Right,' Gippo agreed.

196

'Okay, if that's the case, will they want to be bothered with that bloke's gear in there?' He jerked his thumb at General Gueli's room. He answered his own question. 'Ner, they won't. So what are we going to do? We're going to plant this briefcase, complete with the sleeping beauty's pass, in that little case in Musso's room that you nearly fell over with your big wog plates o' meat.'

Together they hurried down the dark corridor, took the stairs to the second floor and were within the Duce's room once more before the servant collecting the officers' top-boots standing outside the doors for cleaning, had spotted them.

'Phew,' Stevens breathed. 'It must be the bloody luck of the Irish! That was a close 'un, weren't it?'

Gippo nodded.

'Okay, let's get on with it.'

Gippo needed no urging. In a matter of seconds he had opened the little case in the hall. On the big double bed the unsuspecting Duce continued to snore softly. With fingers that trembled ever so slightly, Stevens thrust the briefcase containing the incriminating documents beneath an expensive white silk shirt at the bottom of the case.

Canaris's fate was almost sealed. Now it

197

was up to the Germans to do the rest.

As silently as they had come the two Destroyers stole away back to their waiting comrades.

CHAPTER FOUR

The German *Storch* hovered over the wind-swept mountain at 9,000 feet. In front of the high-winged spotter plane lay Monte Corno. Captain Heinrich Gerlach, Student's personal pilot, was using it as a cover between himself and any curious guard at the hotel below who might chance to glance up and spot the *Storch*. Thirty minutes had passed since he had arrived on the scene and his fuel was running perilously low. Anxiously he scanned the sky for any sign of the gliders. He looked at his fuel gauge. The needle had already reached the halfway mark. He knew he could not afford to cruise around in wide circles looking for Skorzeny and his damned gliders much longer; if they didn't arrive soon he would have to go. His flying time was limited to three and a half hours and if he ran out of fuel over the mountains he hadn't a hope in hell of landing safely.

Once more he slid round the snowy mountain top, using the updraughts caused by the crosswinds to save fuel. Then he saw them. Two sinister black shapes sailing silently through the rarefied air. 'Only two of them!' he exclaimed, talking to himself like most pilots. 'Just two!' My God, he thought, where are the rest? He made a quick calculation. Two gliders – perhaps eighteen men at the most, including the glider pilots and the officers. *Could just eighteen paras pull it off?*

The start of the rescue mission had been planned for midday, but as the twelve big gliders had waited for their tugs, the air had been rent by the pitched wail of an Italian air raid siren. At three hundred miles an hour, twin-engined Allied bombers had come winging in low over the field. Skorzeny and his men scattered wildly. Bombs began falling immediately and continued to do so for fifteen minutes, with wave after wave of RAF Mitchells coming in at tree-top height. When they had gone and the dust had cleared, it was seen that although the field was badly damaged, the gliders had not been touched. The take-off was successful, but an hour later the voice of the towing pilot had come over the phone to announce: 'Regret flights one and two no longer ahead of us. Who's to take over the lead now?' Skorzeny reacted immediately. 'We'll take over the lead,' he replied, and seizing his knife he hacked away at the big glider's canvas wall. Now he could see out properly and direct the glider. An hour later the valley of Aquila came into sight far down below. They were getting close to their objective. The pilot of the towing Henschel let go of the fifty-foot towing rope. The glider lurched down sickeningly. Skorzeny grabbed a metal stanchion and yelled, 'Helmets on!'

The paras behind him prepared for action. Below the hotel was in sight, a white squat horseshoe. Antlike figures were crawling about it.

In the sudden silence, broken only by the hiss of the wind, the pilot swung the plane round in a lazy circle, while Skorzeny searched for the landing strip.

The strip was steep – terribly steep – and littered with boulders. It looked like an abandoned ski-slope. It would be crazy to land on it. But there was nothing else available. The glider started to dive rapidly.

'CRASH LANDING!' Skorzeny yelled. 'Get as near to the hotel as possible!' he added for the pilot's sake. Then he tensed his body for the impact.

The ground raced to meet them. At the very last minute, the pilot jerked the plane's nose upwards and hit the brake flaps. Two thousand pounds of men and material lurched forward, grinding and rending over the stony earth. There was a splintering of wood and ripping of canvas. The barbed wire, wrapped round the plane's skids to shorten the sliding distance, snapped like string. Then with one last mighty heave the plane lurched to a halt.

'The buggers!' Stevens cursed from their hiding place in the bushes, 'they've got us on the hop! It wasn't a para-drop after all.'

'Of course,' Crooke said. 'They couldn't have dropped paratroopers at this height!'

The hotel broke into frenzied pandemonium as the valley echoed with the thunder of the towing planes' engines. Guard dogs started howling; terrified Italian soldiers, some dressed only in shorts, tumbled out of the main entrance of the hotel to where a group of *carbinieri* were frantically trying to set up a machine gun; startled officers, woken so rudely from their afternoon nap, hung out of their windows screaming conflicting orders to the men below.

Skorzeny had no time to consider the astonishing fact that he and his handful of paras had survived the landing. He dropped out of the wrecked glider; behind him was his loyal NCO Otto Schwerdt, sweating under the weight of his equipment.

They were about fifteen metres from the main entrance to the hotel. Above them on the terrace an Italian soldier was standing staring at them in open-mouthed amazement, startled out of his wits by their sudden arrival from the sky. Skorzeny dashed forward. *'Mano in alto!'* he roared, gesturing threateningly with his machine pistol. The soldier's hands shot up. Skorzeny rushed past him. Behind him through the open door the two Germans caught a glimpse of an Italian crouched over a radio transmitter. Schwerdt's big boot shot out. The stool flew from under the radio operator, and he fell to the floor. Next moment the steel butt of Skorzeny's machine pistol crashed down on the radio set with all the strength of his two hundred pounds behind it.

That danger dealt with, Skorzeny cast around for some means of getting into the main part of the hotel. For the little radio room was not connected with it. 'Bend down, Schwerdt!'

Obediently the big NCO did so and using Schwerdt's broad back as a step-ladder, Skorzeny scaled the three-metre high wall which separated the terrace from the hotel. His men followed, while Schwerdt cursed under every fresh weight. Up to now not a shot had been fired.

Skorzeny ran on. Above him on the second floor he caught a glimpse of the well-known bald head and heavy unshaven jaw. The Duce! He was peering out of his window at the amazing scene taking place below him.

'Away from that window!' Skorzeny bellowed at the top of his voice in his best Italian. Mussolini vanished from the window instantly.

Skorzeny ran into the main entrance. A mob of screaming Italians blocked his path. He clubbed about him with his machine pistol. Schwerdt waded through behind him, lashing out on all sides. Beyond them three Italians were trying to set up a machine gun in the hall. One of the German paras booted the tripod from beneath it and it clattered across the polished floor. In the next instant the gunner followed it, skidding across the length of the hall.

Skorzeny galloped up the broad stairs and nearly bumped into two young Italian officers. Behind them he saw Mussolini. He hesitated. The Italians did the same. Behind him Schwerdt came panting up. Two against two, but could he risk shooting it out with the Italians?

Suddenly two grinning heads appeared at the window behind the Italians. On their heads they wore the rimless helmets of the German paras. They were his own men, who had shinned up the hotel's lightning conductor. The Italians saw they were beaten and began to raise their hands slowly.

Skorzeny pushed by them to the window. Another glider was coming in. Gliders three and four had already landed. The courtyard was filled with paras. 'Everything's all right!' he bellowed. 'Mount guard everywhere.'

As he shouted another glider came winging its way in. A sudden gust of wind caught it. It wobbled, then fell out of the sky like a stone. It crashed against a rocky slope and disappeared in a huge cloud of dust and flying debris. Nobody got out.

But Skorzeny had no time for the

accident. From behind he could hear the first sounds of firing. He put his head back in and shouted for the officer-in-command of the hotel.

A bearded Italian colonel peered round a door at the end of the corridor. 'Surrender!' Skorzeny shouted, telling the man that all further resistance was purposeless. The colonel bit his lips and asked for time to consider. Skorzeny gave him one minute. The seconds went by leadenly. Then the Italian colonel reappeared. In his trembling hands he bore a goblet of red wine. With a slight bow and as much dignity as he could muster in his highly nervous state, he said: 'To the victor!'

Skorzeny took a token sip, hoping that the wine was not poisoned and turned to the Italian leader.

Mussolini was pale and unshaven, dressed in a crumpled blue suit, but in spite of his appearance there was no mistaking the joy on his face.

Skorzeny was well aware of the historic importance of this moment, which was going to be the turning point of his whole life; he did it full justice. Clicking his heels together and straightening up to his full height, he barked with military formality,

'Duce, the Führer has sent me! You are free!'

Mussolini, a man who had always had an eye for the dramatic, responded in kind. 'I knew my friend Adolf Hitler would not leave me in the lurch,' he said in fair German and reaching up, pulled Skorzeny's head down so that he could embrace the Viennese giant.

Outside, a strange quiet fell upon the littered plateau as the dusty paras started to spread out the looted white tablecloth as a signal for Gerlach. Exactly four minutes after Skorzeny had hit the ground with the first glider, Gerlach brought his *Storch* in for a tricky landing. All was ready for the last act.

CHAPTER FIVE

It was now three in the afternoon. The Destroyers had crawled as close as they dared to the improvised landing strip – two hundred yards long and sloping downhill. Hidden in the rocks above the strip, they realised that this was how Skorzeny aimed at getting the Duce away from the mountain hotel. Yank, who had once worked for a bush pilot, shook his head dubiously after he had studied the strip for a while. 'It's gonna be one helluva close thing. The pilot will be forced to fly with a north-east wind behind and at full throttle right from the start and he's only got a couple of hundred yards to play with. And, brother, if he ain't airborne by the time he reaches the end of it, it's curtains.' The Destroyers knew he was right. The strip ended in a sheer drop of several hundred feet.

'He's got to make it,' Peters said. 'We ain't come this far to have some Jerry go and kill poor old Musso for us, have we? It wouldn't be fair.'

They grinned at his mock concern, but all of them knew it was well within the bounds of possibility. If the pilot made one slight slip, the whole operation would have been for nothing.

A few minutes later Mussolini came out accompanied by Skorzeny and the pilot. In his hand he bore the case in which Stevens had concealed the papers.

'He's got it with him, sir,' Stevens whispered.

Clad in a shabby blue topcoat, in spite of

207

the heat, and a broad-brimmed felt hat, Mussolini followed the pilot to the plane, Skorzeny, his scarred face serious, towering at his side.

Gerlach swung himself into the cockpit and started the engine. The fuselage trembled as the noise reverberated through the mountains. A couple of paratroopers braced themselves against the wheels, their baggy coveralls flapping wildly in the wind. Skorzeny clambered in under the wing, his vast frame bent double, smiling uneasily at the men he was going to leave behind.

'Goddamn,' the Yank said in disbelief. 'That big Kraut's going too! Hell, he must weigh all of two hundred pounds!'

Mussolini followed, still carrying his little case with the vital evidence against Canaris.

'Take a last look at him,' Crooke said. 'You might never see the like again. One ageing dictator.'

While they watched, Mussolini grabbed a strut and pulled himself into the cockpit, his every movement an expression of his tiredness and resignation. Soon the day would come when the mob would string him up and those same Italian women who had once clamoured for his favours would spread their legs and urinate on his face; but that final indignity was still to come. With difficulty Gerlach pulled the door closed behind him.

He yelled an order to the paras. They relaxed their hold and the little plane began to roll forward. It bumped onwards at 100 mph. The edge of the ravine came closer and closer.

Suddenly, with a tremendous lurch, the *Storch's* right wheel hit a small boulder. The left wing canted downwards and the plane vanished over the edge of the ravine.

'Hell's bells. They've had it!' Peters said. 'I told you they–'

The words died on Yank's lips as the little plane came soaring upwards above the edge of the ravine. A hoarse cheer rang out from the crowd below.

Stevens mopped his brow and breathed out hard. 'Bloody hell, that was a close one, sir. That Jerry pilot must be either brave or touched to have tackled that take-off.'

'Brave, I'd say,' Crooke said quietly.

For a few minutes they watched the plane as it straightened up and set course for the north-east and the field at Pratica di Mare.

The Guardsman broke the silence as the plane became a black dot on the bright blue horizon. 'It looks as if we'd better start making tracks, sir. Them Jerry paratroopers down there look as if they might take it into their heads soon to start poking around the place.'

'You're right,' Crooke said. 'We'd better start getting out of here and looking for that track.' Crooke gave one last look at the glider-strewn landscape, with the bodies of the dead paras trapped in the ribs of their plane. Softly he murmured, as if to himself. 'It looks as if Operation Mincemeat, phase two, is over.'

CHAPTER SIX

'In spite of the base treachery of the scum around Marshal Badoglio, providence – and Major Skorzeny – have ensured that the Duce, Rome's greatest son, will continue to fight on our side.' The shrill voice of the malicious clubfooted German dwarf rose to a crescendo. 'As long as Germany can produce soldiers of the calibre of Otto Skorzeny and his brave men, I, for one, have no fears for the future. Come what may – be it half the world against us – *Greater Germany must and will win this war!'* Joseph Goebbels, the Minister of Propaganda, screamed the last words, *'SIEG HEIL!'*

In the packed hall of the Berlin Sport Palace, the guests invited from all over the Reich for the ceremony to honour Skorzeny broke out into a tremendous roar of enthusiastic acclaim. *'Sieg Heil!'* Brassy electric march music broke in. It was the Horst Wessel song, the hymn of the National Socialist Movement. The audience took it up at once. *'Die Fahne hoch, die Reihen fest geschlossen. S.A. marschiert–'*

Commander Mallory rose to his feet and crossing the deserted Room 39, switched off the radio. 'So much for Goebbels,' he said softly and looked at the Destroyers. Although only Thaelmann had understood the Minister's speech, the applause and wild enthusiasm that had greeted Goebbel's account of Skorzeny's 'historic action for Germany' had sufficed.

'But that about Canaris?' Crooke asked.

'Oh, it worked all right,' Mallory opened a bulky green file on the desk in front of him. 'This is a dossier prepared last week on the Admiral by his rival, SS General Walter Schellenberg, head of Himmler's secret service. It's his aim to combine his service with that of Canaris and make himself boss of the two. This is his complete dossier on the Old Fox's treachery – as he calls it – since 1939. One of our men in his office was kind enough to provide us with it.' He selected a paper from the file and handed it to Thaelmann. 'Perhaps you would be kind enough to translate the last sentence into English for our benefit.'

Thaelmann ran his eye down the paper and began somewhat hesitantly.'"It would have been better for Admiral Canaris to have concerned himself with his own tasks in Italy rather than carry out such sessions with Amé."' He stopped and looked up enquiringly.

'Yes, go on, Thaelmann,' Mallory said. 'Read the bit in Schellenberg's own writing.'

Thaelmann glanced at the phrase written across the bottom of the paper in Schellenberg's own hand. '"*Reichsführer*" – that's Himmler,' he explained. '"*Reichsführer*, this dossier includes the absolute proof of Canaris's treachery."'

'Thank you, Thaelmann,' Mallory said, taking back the paper. 'So you see it looks as if you pulled it off. The Gestapo obviously found our fake dossier. There is no doubt about it, his days are numbered.'★ He broke off suddenly and glanced at his watch. 'And my days will be numbered if I don't get you there on time!'

'Get us where?' Crooke asked.

'Where? Why, we're going to a party given by the chief himself. You're to be the guests of honour in a way, and you're to meet our latest recruits to Naval Intelligence.'

The Admiral's flat was rocking with the sound of Major Glenn Miller's 8th US Air Force band as they entered. Sanding next to the ancient radiogram a pretty red-faced Wren, minus her black tie and showing a little more of her breasts than allowed by King's Regulations, was poised to change the record, when the strains of 'Little Brown Jug' died away.

Mallory and the Destroyers pushed their way through the crowd of guests whose faces they vaguely recognised from their visits to Room 39 and C's offices in Queen

★Admiral Canaris was suspended from duty several months later. On 9 April, 1945, he was strung up by a piece of piano wire at Floessenburg Concentration camp and garrotted to death – for treason!

Anne's Gate. The Admiral stood in the centre of the room, beer mug in his hand, his face flushed above the stiff collar of his full-dress naval uniform. Next to him a thin severe-looking commodore, slowly sipping a small sherry listened tight-lipped and unsmiling to the long involved yarn Godfrey was relating to him.

'What is that which is hanging around the Admiral's neck?' Gippo asked, his eyes greedily sizing up the decoration, as if he were already bargaining on its sale price with some shady backstreet London fence.

'His new decoration, Gippo,' Mallory answered airily. 'He was up to the Palace this afternoon to receive it from the King. Hence the fancy togs.' He accepted a martini from a passing Wren, who was bearing a large silver tray of drinks.

'You mean–' Crooke broke off, not daring to complete the thought.

Mallory nodded. 'Yes, he's going. The officer next to him, Commodore Rushbrooke is to take over the DNI next week. You see one item in that little dossier on Canaris we cooked up in Algiers was unknown to you lot. It was a note to the PM purporting to come from the Admiral, protesting in the strongest terms about any attempt to make contact with Canaris. In essence, the Admiral wrote.' He grinned suddenly. 'Or let's put it like this – we wrote in his name and with his permission, that we should not undertake any form of allegiance with our enemies. If we did, he would be forced to draw certain conclusions in respect of his own person.' He took a sip at his drink. 'You get it?'

Stevens, as usual, did. 'You mean he's got to go now so that Schellenberg thinks he's getting the push because we're dealing with Canaris and the Admiral's against it?'

'Right. Admiral Godrey is going to be made to appear the scapegoat of the oper-ation. An advocate of the "unconditional surrender"doctrine who'll have no truck with the enemy whatsoever. Next week he flies out to Bombay.'

'Bombay?'

'Yes, he's going to be flag officer to the Royal Indian Navy.'

'My God – flag officer!' Crooke said numbly.

'That's right. But don't take it to heart. He's made the sacrifice willingly for the sake of the enigma operation. According to his way of thinking, there'll be no more naval action in the West, but there's a good chance of some real old Nelson stuff in the Pacific against the Japs – and he's looking forward to being in on it after three years in a chairborne job.'

The Admiral finished his story and noticed the Destroyers. He beckoned to them with his beer mug. 'Over here – sharpish, you rogues!' he commanded in his quarter-deck voice. 'I want you to meet your new chief.'

The Destroyers pushed their way through the press of intelligence officers and their girl friends. The Admiral beamed at them, his eyes gleaming a little too brightly. 'There you are, you rogues, looking as if you've been on a rest cure and not out there doing–' He caught himself in time, clapping his big hand over his mouth in mock horror. 'Must keep mum, mustn't I, Commodore. Careless talks costs lives and all that, what.' He turned to the Commodore. 'Rushbrooke, these are the Destroyers I told you about. A real bunch of hard cases and worse, but chaps you can really rely on in a tight corner.' He smiled hugely. 'Your special house troops, you might call them.'

'I see,' the Commodore said without any enthusiasm. 'Actually, sir, I don't believe in private armies.'

Stevens nudged Gippo. 'A proper Charlie, this one,' he whispered swiftly.

'Did you say something?' Rushbrooke asked sharply.

'Yes, sir,' Stevens answered promptly, with a perfectly straight face. 'I said – a nice party, this one.'

Rushbrooke sniffed.

Admiral Godfrey took over. 'Now then, Destroyers, at the end of this week I shall be leaving for foreign parts. It's down to the sea again for the old Jack Tar here.' He winked at them conspiratorially. 'I've been a bad boy, you see, and the powers-that-be are going to get rid of me. I'm obviously a bad influence.'

'Then there should be more bad influences like you, Admiral,' Mallory said, his voice firm, his face earnest. 'We might win this damned war a little more quickly then.'

'Thank you, Miles. That's kind of you. It's precious little I've done really. It's you and your Destroyers who've done all the work and earned me my new gong.' He touched the gleaming decoration at his throat. 'I owe everything to you chaps.' Suddenly he stuck out his big hand. 'Crooke, thank you.' His voice was slightly unsteady and there was a suspicion of a tear in his eyes. 'You've done me proud, you and your chaps!' One by one – Yank, Stevens, Gippo, Thaelmann, Peters – he gripped their hands in his own and pressed them emotionally while they stared up at his rubicund weathered face in embarrassment.

Mallory cleared his throat. His face was still earnest, but there was a suspicion of a grin around his mouth. 'Admiral, I thought it might interest you to know that the Destroyers brought back a little bit of booty from the Italian mission.'

'We did?' the Destroyers asked as one.

'Yes, well indirectly you did. C' – he meant the mysterious head of MI6 – 'is very impressed with them. He wants us to train them for future operations in Italy. He's of the opinion they will make ideal agents for Naval Intelligence.'

The Destroyers looked at each other in bewilderment.

'Them?' Stevens asked, puzzled.

'Yes, them!' Mallory crossed to the other door of the room, which led to one of the flat's bedrooms. He opened it and said, 'Please, come out now.'

The Destroyers waited expectantly.

A handsome dark-haired young man, dressed in a tight-fitting American Army summer uniform with the silver bars of a captain on his shoulder, tripped through the door and paused there, hand poised on his hip. It was Carlo!

'Bloody hell,' Peters gasped. 'The Fairy Queen!'

He smiled delightedly when he recognised the Destroyers and blew them a languid kiss. Admiral Godfrey guffawed hugely. Crooke went a brick red.

'Our new co-belligerent* Carlo Adiorno,' Mallory announced.

Suddenly Carlo stumbled forward, pushed energetically by the other person in the bedroom, a tall peroxided blonde, her dyed hair piled high on her head, her massive bosom threatening to burst the tight serge of her ATS uniform at any moment. She stared at the Admiral's guests aggressively. Suddenly she recognised the Destroyers. Her face burst into a great smile, bright with gleaming gold teeth.

'*Babee!*' she cried. '*My darling babee Steevens!*'

As she rushed forward, arms outstretched,

---

*After Italy surrendered to the Allies, she was classed as a 'co-belligerent nation' and not as an enemy one.

her magnificent bosom jiggling beneath her tunic, Stevens's bronzed face went pale.

'Oh, bloody hell,' he said, *'it's Irma!'*

'Whow!' the Yank gasped and got out of her way, as she advanced on the cockney. 'It's gonna be a hot time in the ole town tonight!'

As the big Italian blonde smothered Stevens in her massive bosom, he began to laugh softly. Peters joined in. Gippo too, a second later. One by one the Destroyers followed until they were all laughing uproariously.

The publishers hope that this book has
given you enjoyable reading. Large Print
Books are specially designed to be as easy
to see and hold as possible. If you wish a
complete list of our books, please ask at your
local library or write directly to:

Isis Large Print Books
Magna House, Long Preston,
Skipton, North Yorkshire.
LD23 4ND

This Large Print Book, for people
who cannot read normal print,
is published under the auspices of

THE ULVERSCROFT FOUNDATION